Pizza Face

Pizza

or, The Hero

Face

of Suburbia

Ken Siman

GROVE WEIDENFELD
New York

I'll always be grateful to Anne Bernays, Walt Bode, Susan Brown-miller, Dennis Cooper, Laura Lindgren, Patrick Peyton, Ken Swezey, and my parents.

Published by Grove Weidenfeld
A division of Grove Press, Inc.
841 Broadway
New York, NY 10003-4793

Published in Canada by General Publishing Company, Ltd.

"It Must Be Him" by Gilbert Becaud and Maurice Vidalin, English adaptation by Mack David (original French title "Seul Sur Son Etoile"), copyright © Ed. Rideau Rouge/BMG Music Publishing France. Used by permission. All rights reserved.

Library of Congress Cataloging-in-Publication Data

Siman, Ken.
    Pizza face / Ken Siman.—1st ed.
        p.   cm.
    ISBN 0-8021-1398-2 (acid-free paper) : $17.95
    I. Title.
PS3569.I472355P5   1991
813'.54—dc20   90-29037
                                                CIP

Manufactured in the United States of America

Printed on acid-free paper

Designed by Irving Perkins Associates

First Edition 1991

10   9   8   7   6   5   4   3

For my brother, John

"Consult the mirror as the courtroom of beauty."

—Achille Bocchi
Inquiries of Bolognese Symbols

Pizza Face

1

ANDY was always looking for the right candidate.

First he started collecting little plaster presidents, four inches high and wrapped in plastic.

Andy and his mother would walk hand in hand to the supermarket that was giving away a different president every week, from Washington to Nixon. Andy would come home, unwrap him, and then stick him on a Styrofoam pedestal with rubber cement. The week they had John F. Kennedy, Andy's mother got an extra one for herself.

When Andy's father wasn't around, his mother would always play the same song by Vikki Carr. It went: "And then the phone rings / and I jump / and as I grab the phone I pray / oh let it please be him / oh dear god / it must be him / it must be him / or I shall die / or I shall die."

The song was on a twelve-inch album, not a 45 single, but Andy never heard what came next. As soon as "It Must Be Him" ended, his mother would lift up the heavy stereo needle and play it again.

While she sang along, Andy would unstick a president

from the pedestal and imagine him phoning her. Eventually, Andy wrote to President Nixon and said, "I think you should pull out of Vietnam and recognize the problems at home," and gave him the family phone number.

But the response was a letter from one of the president's men-in-waiting in charge of correspondence. It said that the president was always delighted to hear from young Americans and that an end to the conflict was in sight.

ONE St. Patrick's Day, Ted Kennedy came to town for the parade. Andy and his mother abandoned his father, who was amazed how the Shriners, such hefty men, could fit onto such little motorbikes. Together, Andy and his mother chased Kennedy through the streets.

When they finally caught up with him, there was nothing to say. He was eating a hot dog. He looked good, though, and his wife was so skinny that Andy's mother wanted to "throw stones at her." It was enough just to know that he used mustard and sauerkraut as condiments.

By the time Andy was old enough to meet some of the candidates on his own, his mother had lost interest. It had come out in the papers that the Kennedy men were untrue. They'd been messing around with tarts with names like Tootsie LaRoux. People were even gossiping about Gerald Ford and Vikki Carr.

"Never again," Andy's mother said, and she broke the "It Must Be Him" record in half. "These men have the morals of alley cats, all the qualities of a dog except loyalty."

For his thirteenth birthday, Andy's mother gave him some books—*The Death of Lincoln*, which had the only known photograph of Lincoln in death, and *Assassination*, a bunch of pictures of the Kennedy murders. Andy stared at the pictures; he had dreams about all the gushing blood.

Still, Andy stayed true. He didn't have much choice. The candidates, through the mail, gave him the only real attention he got. They would always write back, especially at election time, with thank-you notes, buttons, pictures of their families, their wives' recipes, their sincere warm regards and best wishes.

Andy found out there were other men like him, but most of them were a lot older. They belonged to an organization called the American Political Items Collectors and subscribed to a monthly publication, *The Political Accumulator*. The roster of members listed them all by name, age, phone number and address, occupation, and area of interest.

Lars Petersen / 42 / (612) 633-3333 / 4600 Winding Way, Minneapolis, MN / educator / Hubert Humphrey

Don Wasserman / 39 / (212) 976-1616 / 14 Gramercy Park, New York, NY / attorney / Robert Kennedy

These men spent their free time and money getting presidential items from campaigns present and past, back to the olden days. Sometimes they would pay hundreds of dollars for what they wanted; other times fifty cents plus a self-addressed, stamped envelope was enough.

At night Andy would often go through the roster and telephone the ones he thought might be rich, like doctors and lawyers, and try to sell them what he had: old Bobby Kennedy bubble gum cards, Franklin Roosevelt buttons he had stolen from his grandmother's hope chest.

Andy wasn't a thief by nature. He never shoplifted. But his mother made clear that his father's mother wasn't welcome in their home, so her belongings were fair game.

5

"The bitch doesn't pay for rent or groceries, so take what you want from her," Andy's mother said. All she had were some mucusy hankies and the Roosevelt buttons.

The bad feelings between Andy's mother and grandmother probably started even before they were bringing Grandmother down to live with them. She was sitting in the back of the car, next to Andy, and behind Andy's mother, who was in the front passenger—or death—seat.

Grandmother always coughed, but this time it seemed more fluidy. "Pull over," Andy's mother said to his father. "The woman is going to puke down my neck." They were only a mile from home. Grandmother was probably confused. In her old age, she probably thought she was already home. Because in Charlotte, North Carolina, the suburban developments all look the same. They were built by the same company in the same month, for the most part, and it was a rush job because of the sunbelt boom. Families were often accused of trespassing when they only had pulled into a driveway they thought was their own.

But Andy's father didn't pull over. And even though Grandmother kept it down, things were never the same. Andy's father said he knew all along she wasn't going to toss her cookies.

"She didn't have a thing all day, never did touch the Nilla Wafers we got her."

But Andy's mother was convinced that her husband wouldn't have minded one bit if Grandmother ralphed right down her neck.

It was after these kinds of fights that Andy would close the door to his room and call the political collectors, usually on Friday or Saturday nights, when he was sure to get them. Lars Petersen told Andy about the time he met Hubert Humphrey.

"Hubert never fer-gat a name. I tell ya, Andy, if he'd a

stood up to LBJ on 'Nam, he would a made it to the White House and been a dandy prez, a real dandy."

Listening to Lars, Andy couldn't imagine family fights in Minnesota. His voice was so calm and soothing.

Lars and the other men often ended up buying a button or something from Andy. When he cashed their checks, which were always good, he would send off for something, anything that had Jimmy Carter's name or picture on it. It wasn't that Jimmy was real handsome like the Kennedys, it was just that he was so good about writing back.

Their correspondence began in 1975, when Andy was thirteen and the future president was an approachable Jimmy. Andy had sent Jimmy one dollar for his campaign treasury. Andy sent many of the candidates small sums, hoping to start a relationship. But Jimmy was the only one who wrote back personally, the only one who sent him a picture that said: "To my friend Andy, with best wishes, Jimmy Carter."

Andy put up huge pieces of green and white felt in his bedroom, Jimmy's campaign colors. On this felt he would pin his collection. It was reserved for Jimmy Carter.

Andy's parents were not too troubled by this preoccupation. His father would yell about the holes in the newspapers and magazines (Andy would always cut out pictures of Jimmy) and the long-distance phone calls to Plains, Georgia. But his mother thought it was better than his having his mind on "some tart on a record album," and reading periodicals was probably good preparation for the verbal part of the SAT exam. Plus the only TV he watched was the political part of the news, not the more sexy and violent programs.

The North Carolina presidential primary was only a few months away, so a lot of candidates were coming to

Charlotte. Many of these men had written to Andy, or at least their computers had, so he did not think it was being untrue to Jimmy to try to meet all of them.

Andy made a sign that said "Charlotte Welcomes A Fine Candidate." He had an interest in calligraphy and was able to make it look pretty using red, white, and blue felt-tips.

The first candidate to come was President Ford, at the Charlotte Medical Center, the same place where Andy had had his braces put on.

"That's the price of a family car you've got in your mouth," his father had informed him.

It was a pretty small crowd, considering this was the president. Evidently some people were put off at this time because President Ford was being shot at a lot. Still, his mother agreed to take him, and Andy positioned himself so he could shake the man's hand.

"You go ahead, I'll just watch," his mother said.

President Ford got out of the presidential limousine. He said, "How are you all?" to the crowd, trying to be southern. He was surrounded by Secret Servicemen, and behind him were the men running for governor and Congress. Andy shook their hands, too. He didn't want them to feel left out.

At breakfast the next morning, Andy saw President Ford on the front page of the paper. Half of Andy's sign, "A Fine Candidate," and his profile were in the background. It was the 1970s, when men wore their hair over their ears, but Andy's hair winged out on the sides. Sometimes he tried to keep it down with Scotch tape, or his mother would spit on her fingers and try to straighten it for him, but it still winged out.

Andy went to school that day thinking somebody might have noticed that he was in the paper. Even though most of them just read the sports or the comics, maybe

8

one of their parents might have said, "Well, there's a young person your age right behind the president. Now, does he go to your school?"

Andy's heart jumped when his first-period home economics teacher said, "Have any of you all seen today's paper?" but she just wanted to point out some coupons for her lesson on smart grocery shopping.

Andy went into the cafeteria and got his lunch. The cafeteria ladies all had name tags with their first initial and last name. S. Smith, L. Teague. Sometimes they wore rain bonnets when their hairnets were dirty or melted from the hot stove. The ladies scooped up the main course with their serving hands covered by Baggies. A typical lunch was "hamburg gravy" (easy to scoop with the hand), creamed corn, dinner roll, fruit cup in heavy syrup, chocolate milk.

At Christmastime students were supposed to chip in and buy ribbon candy for the ladies who "work so hard to serve us delicious food." But Andy always thought they were kind of mean, so he didn't cough up any money. His homeroom teacher, Mrs. Vault, said it was no wonder he didn't have any friends, where was his school spirit? "You ought to smile more, these are the best years of y'all's lives," she said.

It was awfully hard trying to find a place to sit in the cafeteria if you didn't have a regular table. Sometimes people would say "Leave" to Andy, or just get up and leave themselves. Others would take the retainers out of their mouths and dangle them in front of his eyes.

He finally found a seat next to a boy with a harelip and half a mustache whose nickname was "The Lip." He looked so bad that Andy almost couldn't get his hamburg gravy down. It turned out The Lip's family didn't take the morning paper; his daddy thought it was too left-wing.

At the end of the school day, Andy got on the bus home

and sat in the very front, where all the nervous people sat, afraid of getting hit over the head with a book. When he got off at his stop, he felt a tap on his shoulder. It was Preston, a small, beautiful boy who usually got off at the stop after Andy's.

Preston modeled underpants in the "Dads-n-Lads" section of the Sears, Roebuck catalog. When he was younger, he had been one of Santa's elves and a trick-or-treater on TV advertisements for the Winn-Dixie. Andy liked to look at Preston, but he didn't get much of a chance since Preston was in seventh grade, a year behind him, and always sat in the back of the bus, smoking cigarettes. Up until that day, Preston thought he was the only boy in school whose picture had appeared in any kind of publication other than the yearbook. He wasn't sure how or why Andy had gotten in the paper, but he wanted to find out.

Andy usually ran straight home as soon as he got off the bus, since he never went to the bathroom at school and also was anxious to see if any letters or packages from an American Political Items Collector had come in the mail.

"Wasn't that you in today's paper?" Preston asked.

"Yeah."

"How did you do that?"

"I don't know, I didn't plan it or anything, it just happened."

"Well, how did you know where to go?"

"The candidates send me their schedules."

"Can I go with you next time? My brother has his license and a Trans Am."

"Sure, I guess."

"Great. Tell me the next time somebody famous comes, but make sure we're off the bus like now, okay?"

"Okay."

The next candidate was George Wallace, who came on a Sunday, the same Sunday when Andy was to be confirmed at the Providence Methodist Church. Andy's father didn't believe in God and his mother wasn't sure, so going to church was being on the safe side.

In confirmation class, Andy's mind would wander when Mrs. Register, a lady with a heavy Mississippi accent and cat-eye glasses, explained the history of the Methodists. He lip-synced when she led the class in singing "Onward, Christian Soldiers."

In addition to teaching confirmation, Mrs. Register was the choir director and played the church organ on Sundays. On weekdays she worked in a music store in the mall, selling organs that played automatically, all you did was push a button. Andy wondered if Mrs. Register was worried that the church might buy one of the organs, putting her out of a part-time job.

One girl with whirly blond hair complained that it wasn't fair that Andy didn't sing along with the rest of the class. But Mrs. Register said, "That's all right, 'long as he's got the spirit," and gave him a wink.

Andy thought that since none of the people from his confirmation class went to his school he could maybe make a new beginning and take a girl on a date. He had a lot of extra money from selling buttons; he could take her to a real nice restaurant. But it was pretty much the same feeling he had at school, except this was a weekend. The girls would make faces when he had to stand up and read from the Good Book. They'd giggle or smile when it was a cute boy's turn.

That confirmation Sunday, Andy wore his only real planned outfit. Yellow bell-bottoms, an open-necked slippery satiny shirt with brightly colored parakeets (he chose this one over an Orlon acrylic shirt with a silk-screened photo of the outdoors—trees and lily pads), a puka-shell necklace, a polyester-blend blue sports jacket, blue socks, and earth shoes made of three different shades of brown

11

suede. He told Preston and Preston's brother, Leo, to meet him in the Providence Methodist parking lot around 10:30 in the morning, and then they would all go over to the Northside Baptist Church to see George Wallace.

When the confirming was over, all the young men, now Methodists, lined up in front of the congregation to have their hands shaken by the minister, a tall man who was known as one of the finest tennis players in Charlotte. Then everyone else shook their hands.

"Welcome to the Church, son," a lot of the men said.

Most of the women smiled at Andy and said, "Welcome," but looked at him with sympathy.

Andy noticed that the boys who wore suits with ties and white shirts were getting something he wasn't: the handshakes seemed firmer and the chatter more relaxed.

When the wooden doors of the church opened, Andy heard a radio blaring and a horn honking. It was time to go see George Wallace. Leo's Trans Am was red and had a black widow spider painted on the hood. They played the car stereo real loud and turned it up even more for guitar solos.

Leo, who liked to drive fast, said not to worry about being late. It would be cool if they interrupted a service at Northside Baptist. All those Baptists were just a bunch of rednecks, anyway.

The boys spotted Wallace's entourage as soon as they pulled into the Northside parking lot. Governor Wallace was being lifted in his wheelchair back into a station wagon. Andy rushed over and shook his hand right away.

"Hello there," Wallace said.

Andy knew Preston was all excited, because if he could get in a picture with a famous handicapped person it would help him get the local spokesboy spot on the muscular dystrophy telethon. Now he was angry because there weren't any cameras.

Preston had never even shaken hands with anybody famous except Cloudy McRush, the local TV weatherman, and he approached Wallace, sulking and bashful as he held out his limp hand.

"Well, God bless ya, son," Wallace said as he grasped Preston's hand.

Andy saw this and tried again. All he got was a "Thanks for comin' by."

On the way home, Preston was angry. Andy was afraid this was going to be the last time he would get to ride in a Trans Am. He could even hear Preston's voice over the Led Zeppelin.

"Man, you said there'd be cameras, you don't know shit." For a small, beautiful boy, Preston had a mean voice.

Andy was already a little let down as it was, because Preston had gotten a much warmer response from the candidate.

Preston's brother had both hands on the wheel only part of the time. He played air guitar with his free hand a lot.

"Let's drop him off here," Preston said to Leo while they were on the interstate.

Andy had never hitchhiked before. The instructional films at school said it was dangerous. Andy also thought of the unpopular glee club guy at school who had to hitchhike because he was so abused on the bus. Sometimes students would pull over in their cars to pick him up, and just as he said, "Wow, thanks," they'd peel away.

Andy thought quickly. "I know Jimmy Carter, and he's gonna be here soon. We could go see him. They'll have cameras there for sure." It worked. Preston didn't know who Jimmy Carter was, but he didn't let on.

"Maybe," he said. "Drip."

Every month, Andy got an issue of *Carter News* in the

mail. It told the goings-on of the campaign in a real chatty way, all about the successful trips to Florida and New Hampshire, the Johnny Cash endorsement, Rosalynn getting over her stage fright and making great speeches. The "Coming Attractions" corner of the latest issue mentioned that Jimmy would be at the Charlotte airport that coming Sunday.

Carter News reminded Andy of the "Howdy, Folks" form letters his mother received at Christmas. Every year his mother's friend Mrs. Kilgallen would send a xeroxed letter that detailed the family's activities and tracked the growth of her son, who was Andy's age and had made the wrestling team.

"Marcus shot up three inches and put on some much-needed muscle as per Coach Dodson's instructions." While visualizing Marcus, Andy—lying stomach down on his bed—stained the letter accidentally. He didn't know what the substance was, maybe some kind of pus? He put the letter back in Santa's mailbox with the other Christmas cards. His father examined it under several different lights, wondering exactly what the stain was.

"I must have spilled some milk on it," Andy said.

His father gave it a long sniff and said, "Oh no, this isn't milk."

ANDY wanted to write Preston a note. It had been a bad day at school. In health class they had seen a film about VD and how to avoid getting it. "It cannot be transmitted via doorknobs or public toilets." The film had shown the skin of people who had contracted it. Maurice, the black boy who sat behind Andy, kept kicking his chair and saying, "You ever eaten pussy? You like pussy?"

Andy wanted to see a piece of paper with his and

Preston's names on it. "Dear Preston," Andy wrote. No, Preston wouldn't like the "Dear" part. "Preston, Jimmy Carter will be coming to the airport on Sunday. Do y'all want to go? Andy." Andy's eyes kept glancing at the names, Preston and Andy. He knew he was supposed to communicate with Preston only off the bus, but he couldn't help giving him the note.

Andy sat in the very front seat of the bus so he could give Preston the note as he walked on. Preston and Jerry Featherston from the basketball team got on, laughing while they put cigarettes to their lips. Andy tried to slip the note to Preston, but Jerry grabbed it.

"What's this?" said Jerry. He read the note out loud in a faggy voice. "Who is Jimmy Carter, some faggot from the gay bar?"

Preston said, "I don't believe this shit. I don't know what he's talking about," and slammed his pre-algebra book on Andy's head again and again. Preston was standing up, so the blows were more forceful than usual. They would have to stop eventually.

The bus driver, an older boy from high school, got on. He had a lot of pimples but wore a shirt with a band's name on it that proved he had been to a concert at the coliseum. In other words, he was doing something right. He said, "Man, y'all wanna try pullin' that crap on me?"

"Nah," Preston and Jerry said, and walked to the back of the bus.

"You all right, dude?"

Andy nodded.

Andy's stop came. He was too choked up to say thank you to the bus driver but figured the guy would understand.

Andy ran to his mailbox. There was a padded envelope for him, and he opened it on the spot. Now he had a button that said "Buckeyes for Carter." He went upstairs to his bedroom and pinned it on the green and white felt that covered his wall.

Andy's cat, Mittens, was sitting on his bed in the shape of a meatloaf. Andy took his Jimmy Carter/Mr. Peanut doll and suffocated Mittens for a while, then let her go. She ran down the stairs, meowing like she was in heat. It wasn't that mean of him—Andy had overheard King Burgess, who sat with the guys in the back of the bus, talking about microwaving kittens.

"My mom was real pissed, there was blood and guts all over."

But King's dad owned a chain of appliance stores, so she got a new microwave free of charge.

ANDY'S parents said they'd take him to see Jimmy Carter.

"What happened to the fellows who took you to see Wallace?" his father asked.

"Sunday school." Andy hoped he didn't blush.

Andy put on his planned outfit—the slippery parakeet shirt, puka-shell necklace, and earth shoes. Plus he wore a big pimple on his chin, his first. He remembered that isolated feeling he got in church. He looked at his reflection in the full-length mirror and spit on it. He lay stomach down on the bathroom floor and thought of being beautiful, like Preston. Andy's face was pressed against the bathroom mat, which smelled of old water and pee. He looked again at the mirror, the pimple was redder now, he looked even worse.

Andy took off his clothes. He was about to meet the man of his dreams and looked like doo. He settled for a plain white shirt and pinned on his favorite button, "Jimmy—The Spirit of '76." He put a little piece of

16

masking tape over his pimple, since the only Band-Aids around were concussion size.

Andy went out to the driveway to Scotch-tape a "Carter '76" bumper sticker onto his father's '69 Chevy. Even though the "gold bomb" was all corroded, his father said he did not want the car ruined with a sticker. Just as he was taping it on, Andy saw the Trans Am with the spider on the hood pull into the driveway. He knew he should be angry, but instead it was hard for him to keep from smiling.

"Come on, we're going," Preston said.

Andy's father said, "What about Sunday school? Those boys don't look like churchgoers." It was all right, though; his father didn't want to have to trek out to the airport, anyway.

Preston said they were going because Leo wanted to see the Secret Service agents with their guns bulging under their suits. "Maybe somebody will get shot."

Leo reminded Andy of a boy he knew, Kevin, who got all excited whenever he thought a vacuum cleaner was being used somewhere on the block. To punish him, his mother would lock him outside while she vacuumed, and he would bang his head against the storm door until she let him in.

Leo was already stoned from pot, and hungry. Andy said there would be free Cokes and sandwiches there. He gave both of them a Jimmy Carter poster so they would belong.

In the airport there was a big green-and-white sign with a picture of Jimmy in a work shirt, leaning against a rail fence. The sign said "Let's Elect Jimmy Carter President." Andy had that one, but the sign next to it, "Carter Folks in Oak Room Overlooking Tarmac," was a hand-printed original.

The three boys went to the Oak Room, where everybody else was, along with cameras, food, complimentary brochures. The film crew lights were so bright you could see all the pores in the adults' faces.

"Why is there masking tape on your chin? Are you gonna stick a sign on it?" Preston asked.

"Cat scratch."

Leo wanted to stuff his face with one hand and drink soda with the other, so he made Preston hold his camera. Then Andy and Preston went looking for Jimmy Carter before everybody else got to him. They found him walking out of the VIP lounge. He was smiling broadly and wearing a blue business suit, a bright blue shirt, and an orange tie. Andy got tingles all over. Jimmy, the man from his bedroom walls, had come to life.

Preston was hanging on to Leo's camera and wasn't even taking pictures. He never wanted anything unless he was in it. Preston and Andy handed their signs to Jimmy and he autographed them. Then he took a look at Preston and said, "Would you like to have your picture taken with me?" Preston handed the camera to Andy without looking at him.

Andy squinted through the camera. There was Jimmy, smiling like he did in all his pictures, his arm tightly hugging Preston's delicate shoulder. Andy had never used a camera before, except for an instamatic. He didn't know what to do, which button to press. Jimmy kept smiling and said, "That button there," pointing into the air as if it would help.

Preston looked safe, real comfortable. Andy still couldn't find the button. Then one of Jimmy's aides took the camera from him and told him he could get in the picture, too. Andy took his place next to Preston. Click.

"Y'all hold up those signs, now," Jimmy said.

Preston and Andy followed Jimmy to the Oak Room

18

and heard him give a speech. "I want to be a president who is as good and kind and decent and as filled with love as the American people." Andy wished he could get on a plane with Jimmy and go meet some of these fine people.

Once Andy was sure that Jimmy had gone, he ripped down the "Carter Folks in Oak Room" sign and took it with him.

"I wish you hadn't gotten in that picture," Preston said. "But I would have felt stupid saying anything."

Leo said he noticed a big bulge under one of the Secret Servicemen's jackets, probably an Uzi. He said he made the guy nervous by fiddling with his pockets and looking shifty.

"I fucked those dudes up big time."

They dropped off the film at the Foto Hut drive-through in the mall parking lot; next-day service, two for one. Preston told Andy to lie down in the backseat.

"Cover yourself with that sleeping bag."

It smelled like Preston, so Andy didn't mind. He had to hide because they did not want Terri, the lip-gloss queen of the school and Foto Hut cashier, to see Andy with them. ("Man, I kissed her when she wore root beer," Leo claimed.)

"Hey, y'all, what are y'all up to?" she said.

"I'd like to eat her for lunch," Leo said.

The picture turned out like this: Jimmy Carter smiling with his big teeth, an arm around Preston, whose thin lips went slightly upward. Andy stood next to Preston, his braces showing through a forced smile, although at least the masking tape was barely noticeable. He was hunched over. Andy then realized why Jimmy hadn't asked him to pose first: Andy was just as tall as he was, and it probably wouldn't look right.

Andy's shrine to Jimmy Carter continued to grow during the campaign. He had the photo of the three of them

19

enlarged and sent it to Plains to be autographed. But instead of saying something like "To my friend Andy, who better take a lesson in picture taking," something to show Jimmy remembered, it said just "J. Carter." Andy realized the closer Jimmy was to becoming president, the busier he got.

Once the election was over and the candidates stopped coming to town, Preston stopped seeing Andy altogether. By this time Preston had a picture of himself with the new president of the United States and his own collection of Jimmy Carter stuff. He came over to Andy's one last time; all he wanted was the "Spirit of '76" button. Andy got Preston to wrestle him for it and let him win. He took the button off the felt and gave it to Preston.

"I've gotta go now."

Andy looked out his bedroom window. Leo had been waiting in the driveway the entire time.

Andy would show the photograph of the president to his classmates, but they would say, "It looks like your part was trick photography, you were pasted in." Or, "Who is that cute guy next to Jimmy Carter, isn't that Preston? Y'all don't hang out together."

Andy sent Jimmy the picture again and hoped maybe he would verify it as the real thing. The photo was returned with a note on White House stationery thanking Andy for his support. The signature on the note was fake, just a stamp.

Andy looked at the picture of the three of them again and figured Preston had probably cut him out, it would be real easy to do. Preston had a picture of himself alone with the president. Just the two of them.

2

Ɩɴ high school, Andy's goal was to have the biggest Jimmy Carter collection in the entire country. He even started imitating Jimmy's handwriting and was sure that if he had been a dishonest person he could forge his signature on a campaign brochure and sell it for a profit.

Because of his interest in calligraphy, Andy probably had the most beautiful handwriting in the Charlotte/Mecklenburg school system. The problem was, in high school nobody got credit for good penmanship.

Andy wanted to be able to write in italics. Every Sunday morning he'd get the paper and, like millions of other citizens, turn right to "Walter Scott's Personality Parade," where people asked questions about movie and television stars and other important people. The questions themselves weren't always that interesting, but the way they were printed was: in italics. So Andy would trace over the Qs: *How many Hollywood vixens got their first break on the "casting couch?"* —D.L. Were these people living or just italics, he wondered. What kind of person would write these questions? They sure were pretty italics, perfectly formed, and Andy dreamed of the day he could make them all on his own.

Andy's mother had a job at the Charlotte/Mecklenburg Board of Education and was concerned about Andy. He didn't put much effort into studying, he just sent letters to button collectors and wrote for penmanship's sake. She thought maybe she could convince the board to allow penmanship to be taught in high school for a grade.

"We need a back-to-basics approach," she said. "Have you seen the way young people write these days? It's a damn shame."

She just wanted Andy to get his grade-point average up so he could go to a good college, not the two-year community kind. But nobody was interested in a handwriting class.

"Why teach a child to write pur-ty?" one fellow on the board said, feigning a limp wrist.

"Next thing you'll be asking us to check under their nails," another one said.

Andy wanted his classmates to notice his extraordinary penmanship. But it was real hard to get anyone to sit close enough to notice. His pimples had gotten worse. They had spread to his back and chest, too. He threw away his puka-shell necklace and wore only turtlenecks or shirts buttoned all the way up to hide the painful, festering lumps.

Andy's mother said it was nothing that a good diet wouldn't cure. She would leave out plain yogurt, carrot sticks, bananas, and dry peanut butter on stale whole-wheat bread. Whenever he gagged, he'd wash it down with some sugarless lemonade or powdered skim milk, his choice. "Lay off the pizza and sugar, and the pimples will go away," his mother said.

Andy preferred being called "Pizza Face" over "Monster Face." He tried to start an extracurricular activity called "The Pizza Club," in which students and student teachers would meet in the parking lot after school and sample different kinds of pizza, maybe Pizza Hut one day, Pizza Inn another, and frozen store-bought the next. Then, at the end of each session, all the club members could write comments about the pizzas and compare notes and penmanship. But the only people who showed up in the parking lot were the Lassiter twins, Dwayne and Dana, who also had bad complexions and thought a dermatologist would be there, and Mr. Gimlet, the drivers' ed instructor. Mr. Gimlet told them to get lost; he and Mr. McPherson, the shop teacher, needed the entire parking lot to do pop-a-wheelies with the student-driver cars.

Andy figured he'd try to get attention from something more important, the town paper. He wrote a letter to the editor at the *Observer*, suggesting that instead of sponsoring the annual spelling bee for little schoolchildren, would they consider penmanship contests for virile adolescents?

In a flowing, cursive style he adopted from a Hallmark "Bon Voyage, Skipper" card, he wrote: "Permit me to place a bee in your bonnet. Please picture this: a room packed full of young pupils, just coming of age, putting their wrists to work, Palmer pen in hand, penning prose."

They printed the letter, but in their own regular newspaper type, and they did not show any interest in sponsoring an adolescent penmanship bee.

Sunday after Sunday, Andy kept tracing. He had his fine-point mechanical pencil and onionskin tracing paper neatly set out on his desk and was ready to trace the italics until lunch: *Settle a $5 bet. Is Gavin McLeod of "The Love Boat" and "The Mary Tyler Moore Show" fame any relation to the Leod clan of Bismarck, North Dakota?* And *How many gay linemen are there in the NFL as compared to the phone industry?*

But now there was something different about the questions. At the end of them there was no longer just a set of lonely initials, but full names of people, real people who lived in cities and states. The woman looking for someone famous to sit at the head table at her family reunion wasn't just *A.L.*, but *Anita Leod (Mrs.), Bismarck, North Dakota*. And the guy with the great sense of humor who wanted his phone serviced was no longer *L.G.*, but *Louie Goldbaum, Lima, Ohio*.

Andy hadn't been so excited since he tipped off *The Political Accumulator* about "The Carter Peanut Bag Fraud" a couple of years earlier. Some guy named Mr. Bevacqua was advertising burlap sacks in the *Accumulator* that he said he'd obtained "directly from the Carter peanut warehouse in Plains, Georgia." But Andy found fertilizer in the bottom of his sack and called the *Accumulator* to complain. Once the scam was revealed, Mr. Bevacqua (who owned a fertilizer and tropical fish store) had to write everybody who had bought the sack a letter of apology and refund the five dollars.

Andy got the phone numbers and addresses of the three Goldbaums in Lima, Ohio, from information and found Louie on his second phone call. He crank-called to see how old he sounded: Andy's age, maybe a little older.

Andy crumpled up his onionskin paper, took out a thick sheet of stationery, and wrote:

Dear Louie Goldbaum,

I saw your letter in *Parade* and thought it was great. I never really visualized a phone lineman until I read your letter; I always just associated them with that Glen Campbell "Wichita Lineman" song. I am eighteen years old and collect political buttons. The American Political Items Collectors' Buckeye Chapter is hosting the national meeting next month at Howard Johnson's in Cincinnati. Is that far from you? There is supposed to be a $2 charge,

24

but I hear it's real easy to sneak in for free. I am real tall and have brown hair.

Hope to see you.

Andy

It turned out that Louie Goldbaum lived in an attic. It was his parents' house and they did not think it was proper for a junior-college graduate still to be living in his childhood bedroom. So they let him stay in their attic for a nominal monthly fee.

Louie was twenty-two and had a degree in communications. He once thought this major was a smart decision, given that the area papers were chock-full of help-wanted ads in the telecommunications field. Plus he thought he was quick-tongued and generally a good conversationalist when he had a chance to talk.

It was not until he applied for some of these jobs that he discovered it meant calling people listed in the phone book to try to get them to buy things, usually magazine subscriptions or aluminum siding. Although he was guaranteed an hourly wage, there was no health insurance.

Louie needed health insurance, since it could be dangerous living in an attic, even though it did look pretty much like an ordinary bedroom with its quilted bedspread and stereo system. He was afraid that when he was having one of his nightmares, he could easily roll out of bed and wind up in the kitchen downstairs on account of the attic floor being made out of slats with nothing but pink fiberglass insulation in between.

It was lonely up in the attic too. Louie's parents forbade him to bring his pet cat, Boots, and German shepherd, Stormy, there, for fear that *they* might fall through the pink fiberglass. They were animals, his parents said, and could not tell insulation from the expensive thick purple shag carpeting in the living room and master bedroom.

Louie thought this was unfair, since he had reared Boots and was the only person in the house who'd been nice to Stormy when the creature wasn't housebroken.

Louie's mother, Rita, was ashamed at first, having a grown son living in the attic. But his father, Israel, said a lived-in attic could increase the home's market value. Besides, Don Pope, a family friend, had had a son living in the family toolshed after he was thrown out of military school, and now the boy was making a lot of money as a landscaper. And then there were plenty of people in Cleveland who rented their garages to young people and either parked their cars in the street or had taken the bus to begin with.

"What do you want me to say, Israel? I'm proud that my son lives in an attic?" Rita asked.

It was Louie's first winter in the attic when he realized it would be best to get the fuck out of Dodge and find a place of his own. In the summer he could always pull down the disappearing folding stairs to catch a blast of the central air-conditioning running through the rest of the house. But when winter came, insulation was a priority and the attic stairs had to be folded up the entire time.

Occasionally the stairs would jam when his parents were either out or home with the idiot box turned up real loud, and Louie would be stuck for an extended period of time. He would use the punch bowl his parents had been given as a wedding present for a chamber pot.

Louie would be late for work when he was trapped in the attic, but his employer, Lima Telecommunications, was sympathetic, since he was Lima's best telecommunicator. Fellow employees would just say, "Locked in the attic again, Louie?" more with sympathy than mockery. But nice as his co-workers were, Louie was looking for something more challenging.

His daily routine at work was to go through the Ohio

Bell phone book, usually looking for single women with elderly names liked Enid. A widow or spinster would nearly always be more than happy to talk to a young person like Louie. When he called he'd say their names anxiously:

"Chloris?"

"Why, yes!"

"This is Louie. . . ."

"Who? Speak louder. I can't hear ya!"

"Louie. I used to mow your lawn years ago."

By this time the other party had either hung up because they had always lived in an apartment complex and never had a lawn, or stayed on, blaming a faulty memory for not remembering Louie. Some would imagine Louie as the Little Leaguer or 4-H boy from their past and purchase a subscription to *Modern Maturity* or the large-print version of *Reader's Digest*.

Louie would go home delighted to have made life brighter for a few senior citizens, only to trudge to the attic alone: nobody to see, nobody to call. Sometimes he would call himself and the line would be busy. Sometimes people he'd gone to high school with heard he lived in the attic and called the family phone downstairs and then hung up when Louie picked up, panting.

These were the same fellows who had called him "Louie the Penis" in school. Louie never understood it. He took out his penis and looked at it, then at his face in the mirror. Was he missing something? No, they were just being mean; it was like calling someone "fuckface" or "shithead."

Louie realized he was sabotaging his life by living in an attic. His mattress was big enough to masturbate on, but if he was ever going to have a date over, there would be no room for frolicking on the bed. If anybody was willing to kiss him to start with, that is. Louie figured he was saving a life by not sleeping with another individual. It wouldn't even be a romantic death, it'd be a broken neck on the linoleum kitchen floor below.

But one girl who worked with him said, "Get real, sugar turkey, you're denying yourself a basic part of life."

She was right. Louie was not handsome, but when he was in bed at night, he would take off his underwear and caress himself and wonder if his body felt the same as a really good-looking muscular guy's body would feel once the lights were out or if there was a power failure. When Louie stood up, he realized he had a potbelly. That was what he got for sitting at a telephone all day. But when he lay down, it was firm, not concave, the way it had been in school. He had plenty of chest hair, thick and black. It felt good when he touched himself.

Louie took his hands—piano hands, he'd been told, the only compliment he ever got for his looks—and rubbed them against his face. His skin was clear, he'd never gotten pimples except on his ass, and his stubble was tough, masculine. Alone in his bed he was Louie the Penis, all right, Louie the sexy guy with chest hair and a nine-inch wong; he measured it with his plastic ruler and rubbed it against himself until his belly button was sticky.

As he saved money and got closer to moving out, Louie became more and more conscious of his appearance and began to wonder what it would be like to have sex with others, standing up. Sure, he felt fine to touch lying in a horizontal position in the dark, but when he stood up he realized he couldn't let his pot get much bigger.

If Louie got a desk job at Ohio Bell, he would only get fatter and lonelier; he saw it coming. What else could he do? He was marketable only in the telecommunications field. Fuck. Why didn't he think of it earlier? A man's job?

He'd often noticed telephone linemen. They were so

28

brave. More than one had been electrocuted while trying to restore phone service. Sometimes in the summer they'd provide less dangerous but no less important services, like pulling down a child's kite entangled on a long-distance wire or retrieving a maiden's frightened kitten from a telephone pole.

That was the image that came to his mind: a muscled, tanned body in a yellow helmet and dungarees, tools protruding from a work belt, spikes sticking out of leather boots, muscles bulging as the lineman effortlessly climbed the pole.

These guys had better bodies than the telecom operators or sales reps ever would. Louie was going to be a lineman.

This was around the time *The David Kopay Story* was published in book form. This guy was a big and strong professional lineman from the National Football League who said he was a gay homosexual and what about it, there were *plenty* of others like him. Louie wondered if the two were somehow connected, linemen for the NFL and linemen in the phone company.

Being so knowledgeable about newspapers and magazines from his subscription work, he figured the best person to ask was Walter Scott from "Personality Parade," who seemed to know everything about a lot of people, especially their sex lives. So Louie wrote: *How many gay linemen are there in the NFL as compared to the phone industry?*

A lot of people in Lima were excited to see that one of their own got himself *and* the town mentioned in a national publication. A few came by and dropped off baked goods, even though his question was "a little odd."

To Louie, the most interesting response was a letter that came a few days later from a guy who wanted to meet him. He wasn't a lineman himself, evidently, but he mentioned "Wichita Lineman," which was one of Louie's favorite songs. This guy named Andy wanted to meet Louie at the Howard Johnson's in Cincinnati. Louie was glad to have something set up for a Saturday. And a room at the HoJo would be better than the attic.

THE button convention in Ohio would be the first time Andy really got away from home, excluding the Teen-aged Democrats' convention in Raleigh, which didn't count, since (a) it was in state and (b) he had an awful time.

Andy's mother didn't want him to spend hundreds of dollars to go to a button convention. Didn't he have enough buttons already? But he made enough money selling them that he could afford the trip on his own; she couldn't stop him.

It was the first time Andy had been on a plane. When he saw that all the other passengers had fine leather bags, he felt real self-conscious carrying all his underwear and pimple stuff in a Winn-Dixie grocery bag. He had to carry it from the bottom, since the cap to his rubbing alcohol wouldn't screw on tightly. It leaked out and smelled the whole front cabin up.

"I'm sorry, young man, you can't bring liquor on the plane," said the flight attendant.

"Oh, it's just for my face."

"*What?*"

"I mean, it's rubbing alcohol."

"Uh-huh," and she made it a point not to give him the complimentary almonds.

Andy took a cab to the Cincinnati Howard Johnson's and tipped the cab driver five dollars. The motel was clean and reasonably priced and full of vacationing families making pit stops for the many flavors of ice cream with bits of ice in it.

Andy was excited about meeting all the fellow political-item collectors he had talked to on the phone and over-charged for buttons. Maybe he'd meet that Louie guy, too. They could get alcohol cocktails in the lounge if they didn't get carded. But maybe Louie was twenty-one.

To get to the meeting room you had to walk through the dining area. The people who weren't eating ice cream in little silver dishes were celebrating the weekend with late-morning breakfasts of griddle cakes and coffee with free refills.

Just outside the restaurant a folding table stood on an orange carpet that spread into a meeting room with tur-quoise walls. There was a stack of "Hello My Name Is" stickers. Andy wrote his name on one and stuck it on his turtleneck. He hoped Louie would come and find him.

As soon as he'd stuck the tag on, a little man who barely came to Andy's neck said, "How are ya, partner?" It was Lars Petersen! Lars was probably in his mid-forties and wore a short-sleeved plaid shirt, sleeveless vest, and poly-ester pants, the kind without belt loops. He had wire-rimmed aviator glasses on his face. He seemed glad to see Andy but never looked him in the eye; instead he kept staring at his name tag and talking as if he were on the phone.

"Looks like ya got the best of me on our last swap; that Humphrey-Carter button is scarcer than hen's teeth!"

Andy looked around the room. Almost everyone there was a man, and everybody, man and woman alike, dressed pretty much the way Lars did. Nobody there was real handsome. Andy was the youngest.

The whole place had the same general feeling as his bedroom, but with folding chairs and tables in place of a bed. There were pictures of politicians all over—Nixon,

Roosevelt, Kennedy, Eisenhower, Goldwater. There weren't that many of Jimmy Carter, since he was becoming less popular as the price of gas increased.

Trust and fellowship were everywhere that day at Howard Johnson's. Checks were exchanged freely, identification was never required.

Andy bought a Jimmy Carter ceramic tile and thought about getting his mother a full-color Jackie Kennedy button, but he didn't want to bring up old wounds.

Finally, toward the end of the day, a short, kind of fat fellow who needed a shave and had on a sweatshirt that said "Chevy" came by.

"Hello, I'm Louie from Lima."

"Oh, hi, it's great to meet you," said Andy.

Louie looked like he belonged there, even though he was younger than everyone except Andy. Now that Andy saw him, he tried to remember why he had written to him in the first place.

"Well, what do you think of all these buttons?" Andy asked.

"Why, I've never seen anything like this."

They went into the restaurant. It was all-you-can-eat fish night. Fish was the only fried food Andy's mother encouraged him to eat. She said it would keep him from getting a goiter. Since he got big oozy pimples no matter what he ate, Andy figured he could enjoy some french fries, too.

"I'd like the fish platter with fries and a Pepsi, please."

"We have no Coke or Pepsi, only HoJo cola," said the waitress.

"Beg your pardon?"

"Only HoJo cola."

"Um, okay, HoJo cola."

"Ditto," said Louie, "with extra cocktail sauce *and* tartar sauce."

"So, Louie. Do you have a favorite president or anything?"

"Never really thought about it. Nixon was okay, I guess. One thing's for sure, this Carter is for the birds."

Andy didn't want to argue, the fish hadn't even arrived yet.

"So, are you in school?" Andy asked. "Or do you have a regular job?"

"Telecommunications," Louie replied. "Right now I'm working on becoming a lineman for Ohio Bell."

"You were serious in that *Parade* letter?"

"Yeah, what did you think?"

"Oh, I don't know. It was just interesting, I guess."

Louie thought that Andy was pretty homely, especially with all his pimples, but his height was somehow appealing. Louie remembered his trick of turning the lights out. Those bumps wouldn't be so bad in the dark.

Louie ordered some peppermint ice cream for dessert and convinced Andy to try some. He thought it would be nice if they didn't have fish breath.

"It's a drive to Lima, mind if I spend the night?"

"No, sure," said Andy.

Andy fumbled for his room key. "After you," he said to Louie.

They put on the TV and Louie reclined on the bed.

"Too bad the vibrator's broken," he said.

"At least the ice is free."

"Say, Andy, aren't you hot with that thick shirt on?"

"Nah, I've always got a chill. I'm really high-strung."

Louie took off his sweatshirt anyway. He had on a V-neck T-shirt with holes in it. He had planned it that way; the holes and the V showed how hairy his chest was.

Andy was sitting cross-legged on the floor and saw how tight Louie's jeans were and what a big bulge he had in them. Maybe that's why the waitress charged them for only one HoJo cola.

Louie didn't have any buttons to wrestle over, and even if he had, Andy would not have wanted to.

They watched a movie, *Grand Theft Auto,* and Louie made car noises and pretended to be operating a stick shift in the chase scenes.

Andy rubbed some pimple cream on and tossed one of the pillows to the floor.

"I can sleep on the floor, Andy."

"No, really, you live in an attic. Enjoy this."

When he got a whiff of Andy's pimple ointment, Louie lost all interest. Andy smelled like chemistry class in high school.

When Louie left the next morning, Andy pretended to be asleep.

His ointment had bleached white a large patch of the orange carpet, and he was worried someone from HoJo's would ask him to pay for the damage. He left in a hurry.

Andy hunched down and looked at himself in the airplane's bathroom mirror. He wondered if he was a tall, pimply version of Louie, if people looked at him the way he looked at Louie. Then a heavyset lady walked in; Andy had forgotten to slide on the "Occupied" sign.

"Oh, I'm very sorry," she said.

She hadn't interrupted anything.

3

ALTHOUGH Andy was not an athletic fellow, his mother thought it would look good on his college application if he was on some athletic team, and not as team manager. Plus she wanted to gentrify the family some. The answer was tennis.

There were four ways to play tennis in Charlotte.

The most prestigious was to join the club for rich southern people. It had what looked like an antebellum mansion for a clubhouse. It hosted national golf tournaments—the only time Yankees were allowed in the place.

Not much different from that was one in the same neighborhood that also cost a lot of money to join but that did allow people with northern accents, usually bank vice-presidents, but no Jewish people.

Third were neighborhood clubs, which anybody who could afford the membership fee was allowed to join.

Then there were the public courts, where people wore street clothes and drank wine straight from the bottle between games.

Andy's family joined the third kind. They took lessons together, the three of them.

Les, the tennis pro, had a deep tan and a mustache. Even when he sweat, his hair stayed perfectly in place. The ladies took lessons from him and said they were beginners, even if they weren't, so they'd have more time with him. "Now, Les, how do I hold this silly old thing?" Andy would watch as Les's strong, hairy hand would press itself against the delicate wrist of a fawning woman his mother's age.

Andy's father was uncoordinated and would often hit balls clear over the fence and into the street, which the club tried to hide with a row of scrubby trees. But at Cedar Forest, as the club was named, players could still hear car engines and teenagers shouting "Fuck up!" just as they went to serve.

After every lesson Andy's mother would be furious because she had been embarrassed in front of Les. She said her husband was humiliating her on purpose. He couldn't do anything right. He wore socks that either were the wrong color (not white) or went up too high, for example.

Once, riding home, she said, "Why did you bring those G-D orange balls? Only trash uses them!"

Andy's father finally pulled the car over to the side of the road and said, "Get out."

After that, Andy and his mother went by themselves. All they had was each other.

Andy's mother wore a short tennis skirt to the club, white, all cotton. Andy thought she looked good. From her old black-and-white pictures, he could tell she had been kind of fat and homely and flat-chested before she was married. But as she got older she ate a lot of melba toast and small-curd cottage cheese and worked hard on her deep tan. It was always the good-looking girls in high school who got fat and lumpy afterward.

Andy's mother bought him fashionable tennis clothes, with alligators on the shirts, the shorts, even the socks. Sometimes when Andy and his mother were rallying on the court there would be two boys playing on the next court, grunting after every serve. Andy would get an awful feeling. They wouldn't even say "Hey" when they were standing right next to him by the vending machines.

Then Andy's mother got mad at the tennis pro for some reason and started using the public courts, even though they had three months left in their Cedar Forest membership. Once when she was playing with a black lady from work, she saw a young fellow, a college boy, who was giving a lesson on the next court. She got his number and said to Andy, "Maybe he can teach you. Tryouts for the school team are only a month away, right? This boy seemed to know what he was doing."

Andy fantasized about making the tennis team, celebrating with people he did not know yet. He couldn't see himself in a varsity jacket, though.

Tim turned out to be a nice-looking boy, just as Andy's mother had said. He lifted weights for a more powerful serve, and it showed in his arms. He would pull into Andy's driveway and honk the horn. Andy never made him wait.

Andy was a lot taller than Tim; that felt awkward, since he was physically weaker and inferior in every other way. Andy's mother would write out checks for ten dollars, and Andy would give them to Tim when the hour was up. He wished somebody from school could see the two of them together. They didn't have to know he was paying for it.

Andy played the best ever with Tim. He hoped Tim would ask him out for a beer, so he would volunteer,

"Wow, I've never been there," when they drove past a bar Andy knew was popular among people around his age. Then Andy realized that wasn't included in the ten dollars.

Tim said he thought Andy had a shot at making the team, and he'd put in a good word for him. He was drinking buddies with the coach's brother.

"Good luck, guy," he said when he dropped Andy off for the last time.

When the first day of tennis tryouts came, Andy wore his tennis clothes underneath his regular outfit so he wouldn't have to undress in front of anybody. In geometry class the teacher liked the parallelogram he had drawn on his homework assignment. "Come to the board and draw it real big for all of us," she said.

Uh-oh. Andy had traced the thing from the encyclopedia. He got to the board and knew he couldn't do it. When his back was to the class some girl said, "Ewwww gross, he's got two pairs of pants on," and everybody laughed. "Duh." Andy looked at the geometry teacher, and she nodded for him to sit down. At least it saved him from having her know he had faked it. Think positive. He didn't want to get too upset before tryouts.

Andy went to the gym locker room after school. It took him only ten seconds to get ready. The other boys were taking off their shirts and pants. Most of the boys going out for tennis were skinny and pretty and rich. They had smooth chests. Some of the other guys in the locker room were going out for track. They were hairier and more muscular, like Rich, who threw the shot put.

Andy had first noticed Rich back when they were in junior high school. Even then, he had big muscles and students were saying he had affairs with the young pretty teachers. Andy would always try to position himself in the cafeteria so he could see Rich's biceps expand as he brought a meaty sandwich to his lips.

Now Rich was standing right next to him, naked except for a jockstrap. Andy didn't want to look; he was afraid of what might happen. His knees were weak.

Andy played his first set and was ahead 5–0, but he lost the next seven games in a row. Waiting for another match, he spotted a guy running laps around the courts with the track guys. His hair was black, his skin was olive, and his tank top was yellow.

He said "Hey" to Andy through the chain-link fence but never broke his stride. Maybe he thinks I'm somebody else, Andy thought.

A couple of weeks later, the tennis team members were announced at the end of practice. Only two of the sixteen who went out didn't make it. One was the guy who had a back brace and hoped to make it on school spirit. The other was Andy.

Andy was relieved to finally be able to go home right after school so he could go to the bathroom. It had been a real drag holding it through an entire school day and then two hours of tennis practice.

He was getting into the "gold bomb," which his father had let him use, when somebody said, "Wait up." First he thought it was the guy with the back brace. Nah, it wouldn't be him, he didn't like Andy's cynical attitude. It was the real good-looking guy with the tank top, from the track. He was limping.

"Can you give me a ride home? I don't live far."

"Okay."

He pulled up the bottom of his tank top and wiped his brow with it. His skin was so beautiful, so smooth. There was a little bit of hair around his navel, barely enough to make him masculine.

"I'm Ryan Perez." He held out his hand.

Andy hoped his wasn't sticky.

"Are you okay?" Andy asked.

"Yeah, I fucked up my ankle, so I'll have to miss practice for a week or so."

Ryan was new; he had gone to Catholic school in New Orleans.

Andy started the car. It died. He tried again.

"This happens all the time."

Ryan went under the hood and said something about an idler. Whatever, he touched a car part.

It started.

"Did you make the tennis team?" Ryan asked.

"Nah."

"Bummer. You seem to be okay about it."

"It's just as well." Andy kept braking in the middle of the street.

"Did you run over somebody recently?"

"No, why do you ask?"

"You drive like my dead aunt."

"Was she a hit-and-run driver?"

Ryan laughed. He took out a Baggie from his gym bag and started rolling a joint.

"What are you doing?" Andy asked.

"What do you think? This pain is killing me."

"Just not in the car, okay?

"What are you worried about? You drive like a geriatric, you're not gonna get pulled over."

"No, it's my father."

"What, are we going to pick him up now?"

"No, he'll be able to tell."

"*How?* I won't leave anything in the ashtray."

"He has a great sense of smell."

"All right, man, whatever."

They pulled into the circular driveway in front of Ryan's house, which looked a lot like Andy's.

"Do you want to come in?"

"Why not?"

It was like any other home in Charlotte, except maybe the carpeting in the foyer was thicker and the coatrack was made out of deer feet.

In the den were photos that appeared to be Ryan in different stages of his life.

"Aw, man, don't look at those."

Ryan's mother came out of the kitchen.

"Hi, Mom, this is . . ."

"Andy."

"This is Andy."

Ryan's mother looked like him, and her hair was all done up. She was wearing a dress even though she wasn't at work. The TV was on.

"Aren't you home early, honey?" she said in a sweet southern voice.

"My ankle's fucked up, Mom."

"Ryan!"

"Sorry."

"Let me take a look at it, baby."

"I'm *fine*, Mom."

He shut her up quick. Andy thought he was watching something private.

"Can I fix you boys something to eat?"

"In a few minutes, Mom, we'll be real hungry then." Ryan smiled at Andy.

Andy walked up the stairs behind Ryan. It took a while, on account of his limp.

Ryan's room had dumbbells and a chin-up bar. His dirty clothes were all over the place; he wore boxer shorts.

Andy wanted to watch Ryan exercise, but he was too embarrassed to ask.

They sat on his bed. Ryan took out his Baggie again.

"You've never tried this, have you?" He put some of the weed in a rolling paper. It looked like oregano.

Andy remembered a guy who was once given some oregano rolled as a joint and was told it was marijuana. "Come on, dude, try it." The guy pretended he was high and started talking about everything changing colors and about being happy as a lark. Then all the guys who were in on the joke started laughing their heads off. They told him he was "high" on oregano from the Pizza Inn and how they had uncapped all the oregano and garlic salt jars so the next sucker who wanted his dish to have more zing would have a ruined meal instead.

Andy looked at the black hairs on the back of Ryan's olive hands as he rolled the joint. "You're sure this is okay?" Andy asked, unsure about what he even meant.

"Man, you're getting paranoid before you've even touched the stuff. You're going to be a lot of fun, I can tell."

Andy took a puff, blew it out.

"Hold it in," Ryan said.

He did, and felt real close to Ryan right there on the bed.

Ryan's mother came in with cheddar cheese and saltines and Cokes on a tray. If the room smelled weird to her, she didn't let on.

"Y'all enjoy this."

"Thanks, Mom."

"Thank you, Mrs. Perez."

"So," Ryan asked, "what do you want to be?"

"I don't know, maybe go into politics or something."

"Why don't you run for student council?"

Was he serious?

"Nah, I'd rather work in an adult campaign. How about you?"

"I want to be a doctor."

When Ryan went to the bathroom, Andy looked at some of his medical books, the ones with pictures, and

42

saw a baby being born. It was being pulled out of the woman's opening with some tongs.

Andy's mother had once told him, "The man puts the seed in the woman's hole," but he never knew it looked like this. Andy felt sick to his stomach. Maybe it was the pot.

He showed the picture to Ryan.

"I thought the baby came out of the woman's stomach," he said.

"Who brought you up, man?"

Andy had to go home for dinner. He wasn't that stoned, but still he was worried. He didn't want to get pulled over by a cop and have his father's insurance rates increase.

He put on his brakes even more than usual. A lot of people honked their horns as they passed him and yelled things he couldn't hear.

In his new frame of mind, Andy's family seemed the same, maybe a little more uptight. His grandmother was in the kitchen breaking wind while she peeled potatoes with a knife, even though she knew the family owned a vegetable peeler.

For dinner there were cold stewed tomatoes, white codfish with bones (room temperature), watery mashed potatoes, powdered skim milk, and dry whole-wheat bread. Grandmother had to eat upstairs or outside on the patio because of her internal problem. Andy's father suggested they play music loud enough to mask the unappetizing sound and eat together as a family, but Andy's mother said no.

Andy avoided sitting by the window. Dinner was served just as the sun was going down, and his father had remarked that it gave Andy's acne a purplish tint.

Andy's mother asked him what he had done that day. He was too embarrassed to talk about Ryan, so he pretended he got a button in the mail: "Ohio Senior Citizens Back Carter."

"Whatever became of that fellow who lived in an attic in Ohio?" his father asked. "Are you two still writing?"

"No, not since the button convention. He's kind of weird."

"What do you expect from someone who lives in an attic? He's a loser," his mother said.

Even though Andy didn't care for Louie, he felt a need to defend him.

"I think he's planning on moving out real soon."

"And how old is he?" asked his mother.

"I don't know, twenty-one or something."

"See what happens if you don't study hard? That's how you'll wind up, in a G-D attic."

"God, he wasn't *that* bad off." Andy was afraid the conversation would turn to his grades and how he needed to bring up his SAT scores on his next try.

"How would you like to be living in our attic when you're that age?" his mother said. "It's so sad, I feel sorry for his poor parents."

"You don't even know his parents."

"I don't have to, it's a universal feeling. Is that how you want to wind up?"

"It would be okay if it was well insulated. Maybe you can take in a boarder up there when I go to college."

"It's not something to laugh at. It's sick, sick, sick."

Andy looked down; the sun had struck his face.

"Were you picking at your face today?" his mother asked.

"No." He had been, though.

"I see an open sore," his father said.

"Let's have a closer look," said his mother, who got out of her chair.

"May I be excused? I think I'll go up to the attic."

"Sick! Don't pick!"

Andy would usually go upstairs when the conversation

reached this point and masturbate or play a record, but he called Ryan instead. There weren't any other Perezes in the Charlotte directory.

"My parents are working my nerves."

"Come on over."

Andy was starving, so he stopped at the Pizza Hut and got a large pepperoni, and a big bottle of Coke at the Piggly Wiggly.

Ryan's mother opened the door and seemed real friendly. She sent Andy straight upstairs to Ryan's room, apologizing for its messiness. "I hope you don't think it's a reflection on me."

Ryan was wearing only a pair of running shorts. He was propped up against a pillow, his arms behind his head, watching a rerun.

"It's the pizza boy," Andy said. "Have you eaten?"

"No. Me and my parents eat at different times, so I usually don't eat till later, when my father's done." Ryan said his father was a businessman who worked in one of those glass office complexes downtown.

He rolled a joint. It was amazing that Ryan could smoke pot like this and watch TV and still be good enough in school to think about being a doctor.

"Here you go. Hold it in longer this time."

Andy did, then coughed. His throat burned. He was doing something right, finally.

When Andy passed it back, he let his hand slip over Ryan's. Ryan didn't seem to mind.

"You nigger-lipped it!" Ryan said.

Andy had gotten saliva all over the joint. He'd fucked up.

But then Ryan went and took a hit anyway and passed it back.

"Come on, Andy, let's go meet some babes."

There was this beach club with sand on the dance floor Andy had heard about but never been in.

Ryan put on some jeans and went to the bathroom to comb his hair. Andy went with him, to check his face. It was a long bathroom with a wide mirror and bright lights and shag carpeting. Ryan's towels were all over the place.

Andy looked in the mirror, saw the two of them together for the first time. He knew he looked bad, but he had never seen someone standing so close to him before.

The beautiful olive skin. The red cratery skin. The awkward stooped posture. The perfect smooth chest. He felt lust and disgust. He couldn't go out looking like this. Before, he thought going out with a good-looking guy could only rub off on him, make him look better.

"I think that pot made me sick," Andy said. "I better just go."

"Just take some aspirin, lie down for a while. I can wait."

"No, really, I might lose it."

"Well, shit, I hope you feel better."

Andy didn't brake this time—he drove the fastest he ever had. He almost ran over the school midget, a "physically challenged young man," who was in his twenties and still only a junior in high school. He was riding a tricycle on the side of the road.

He'd probably have been doing the guy a favor.

4

ANDY'S French teacher was a man who wore black bell-bottomed jumpsuits, silk shirts, and black platform shoes. His name was Jean-Paul. His God-given name was John and his middle name was Paul. He was from Fuquay-Varina, North Carolina, but he did not have even a trace of a southern accent. He spoke the same way he smoked his Virginia Slims 100's, slowly and elegantly.

Andy liked him right away when he told the class that his favorite actress was Angie Dickinson. She was the star of Andy's favorite show—which he was forbidden to watch—*Police Woman*. Andy's mother hated her because newspapers said she had had an affair with John Kennedy, a married man with two children. Andy had to sneak into his grandmother's room to watch the show on the old black-and-white set. He had trouble hearing Angie over Grandmother's snores, but it was still worth it. At least Grandmother wasn't breaking wind.

Andy liked Jean-Paul even more when one day after class he said, "There is one word for Charlotte: *redneck*."

Students laughed in Jean-Paul's face and called him a

faggot within hearing distance, but he wasn't fazed. He kept dressing in a "style-conscious" manner. Some of the students who were really hung up on Jean-Paul's sex life found out he lived with a hairdresser from the mall. They found his address even though it wasn't listed in the phone book and wrote "Jean-Paul sucks the big one" in pink paint on his driveway. The artistic one of the bunch drew a large penis, also in pink.

One Friday night the group drove over to see if their "artwork" was still there. It had been blacked out for the most part, but one of them shouted, "You can still see some of the dick!"

The big assignment in French class, worth three test grades, was to make or produce something that pertained to French culture. Jean-Paul recommended dramatic skits, perhaps a reading from *Le Petit Prince*. But most students made French food.

Cassandra Lybrand brought in some french toast topped with jam made in France instead of maple syrup. Princess Mayfield, whose father had served in the armed forces during World War II, brought in a tin of potted meat that had been rationed to him in France. "*Surely* you don't expect us to eat *that*, Mademoiselle," said Jean-Paul.

"I guess not," said Princess, who got a C minus.

"Andy, your presentation is tomorrow, *n'est-ce pas?*"

"Yes sir."

"Pardon?"

"I mean, *oui.*"

Andy was going to bring in a Xerox of a Charles de Gaulle poster and make a speech from the French Resistance. But that very night he saw a picture of Carolina ("C.C.") Cheshire, the North Carolina governor's wife, holding a plate of "Chocolate Mousse à la Carolina," and that changed everything.

48

Right away, his feelings for her were special, like the way you feel for your first pet or favorite hit record. She was on page 1C of the *Observer*, in the "Carolina Living" section. Carolina was in full color. Her acorn-brown hair was piled high, nearly up to providence, and made her a little taller than her husband, Governor Lucius Cheshire—even though his own pompadour was pretty big, too.

Her skin was pure white, like a bar of fancy hotel soap that had never been used. Her fingernails were crayon-red and sharp, perfectly formed, and she was skinny as a rail—you could tell she didn't eat her recipes. She was sharing them just to be kind, and to help her husband get elected to the United States Senate.

The recipe called for sponge cake—"No need for anything fancy," she wrote, showing she wasn't a highbrow, which was important to do, especially in an election year. "Just dribble some melted chocolate bars—Hershey's, Nestlé's, whatever—over the sponge cake, plop on some Cool Whip, refrigerate, and *voilà*."

"That means 'presto' to you and me," the governor was quoted as saying.

Andy followed the recipe closely and got a B minus.

"You would have done better had you made an entrée or a more indigenous dessert, perhaps *crème caramel*," said Jean-Paul.

Andy had been interested only in presidential candidates up to this point, but now he wanted to know more about Carolina Cheshire and her husband.

He phoned his button friends, some of whom lived in Washington, D.C., and knew about men who ran for high offices. Between them and Lucius Cheshire's campaign literature, he found out an awful lot about the First Couple of North Carolina.

Lucius was only forty when he was elected. He had always been achievement-oriented. President of the state

Teen-aged Democrats at age twelve, the first preteen to hold the office; regional director of the 4-H Club at fourteen, state senator two years after law school; lieutenant governor; governor. Now he had his eyes set on Washington, D.C., to be a "U-nited States senator."

"I'm seriously thinking of running for the U-nited States Senate, but first I want to talk to my lovely wife and three children and the people of this great state before I make up my mind. Washington's chock-full of asinine folks, and I think we could use some Carolina common sense up there."

Andy's mother was impressed with the governor's background, but she found him too pretty and his wife too vain. "All she cares about is appearances, I can tell by the looks of her."

Yet Andy's mother liked something about the governor. "Look what *he* did when he was your age," she said to Andy. "He wasn't feeling sorry for himself because he got a pimple on his face."

"That's probably because he didn't have a pimple on his face," Andy replied.

Flawless as Governor Cheshire appeared to be, the word was that one thing could hold him back: his wife. He had to be constantly in control of her, have her in his—or one of his aides'—sight at all times.

Carolina Cheshire was born Caroline DeWitt, to a fine family in Memphis, Tennessee. She met Lucius at a regional 4-H convention when they were both teenagers, and they continued to court in college and finally married when he was in law school. Lucius didn't have an income, so he let Carolina teach school under two conditions: one, she would quit as soon as he graduated; and two, she could teach only grade school—he didn't want any pubescent boys ogling her while she read aloud from *The Grapes of Wrath*.

On their honeymoon night, the story went, Lucius was already thinking about his political career and sweet-talked Caroline into changing her name to Carolina. This would make up for her being originally from Tennessee.

At first she was reluctant to change her name. Her family was proud of its Tennessee roots. But Lucius was a smooth talker, and handsome to boot, and while delicately kissing her nipples he said, "Come on, precious, just change one little letter for your little man." He moved gently down her body with his tongue. "You'll still end with a vowel."

"Oh, hell," she said, and he knew he had her.

Now, at campaign rallies, Lucius could tell the crowd: "Why, I'd only marry a woman with a name as pretty as our state, and folks, I found her."

Carolina got bored being a politician's wife and started calling herself C.C. to show her independence. When Lucius was lieutenant governor, she had to meet with all the groups the governor's wife shunned: macramé clubs, people who had turned a hundred, mimes from the state fair, elementary school students singing carols in shopping malls.

C.C. got lonely, too. Lucius was always running to something or for something.

"I deserve better," she told her best friend and chief assistant, Flo Alpha. "I'm an attractive woman. Hell, a lot of those teenage boys I meet down at those pro-reading meetings fancy me."

Flo Alpha was six feet tall, with flaming red hair. "You can't get this color out of a bottle, baby," she would say.

Lucius didn't like Flo. "I just don't trust this bitch," he'd tell his staff. "She's trouble, you know. She'll put wild ideas in Carolina's brain."

Flo's nickname was "Bless Your Heart," because she was always saying that to everybody. Whenever she was bored or someone was going on about livestock ("Have you noticed, ma'am, the shorter the incubation and gestation periods, the smaller the critter?"), she would speak for herself and C.C. and say, "Well, bless your heart." They'd be out of the conversation and into the state-owned sedan quick as all get-out without seeming the least bit uppity.

In a state used to political wives who were proper and fragile (citizens had been encouraged to call the last governor's wife "Grandma"), C.C. and Bless Your Heart got the kind of attention usually reserved for college basketball heroes.

Sometimes they would drive in to towns in a rented convertible and you could see their hairdos—C.C.'s chestnut bouffant and Bless Your Heart's red mane—blowing in the wind as they whizzed on by, often going over the speed limit. C.C. would get uptight about breaking a state law; after all, she *was* the governor's wife. But Bless Your Heart would say, "Calm down, C.C., they're not going to pull over the First Lady of the state."

They became the center of attention no matter where they went and were invited to a lot of the functions the governor couldn't make. Sometimes they were even the first choice.

"Why, they look like New York models, but they're just as friendly as can be," one Morganton citizen remarked to another, who nodded and said, "You know, you're right."

An informal *Fayetteville Times* poll conducted at "pig pickin's across North Carolina" showed C.C. and Bless Your Heart to be two of the most beloved women in the state, right behind Misty Freeway, whose husband, Humpy, owned Raceway 600.

Lucius was not about to be overshadowed by anyone, especially a "nobody" like Bless Your Heart. He'd spent his entire life plotting his rise, and that "bitch" had gotten lucky only by getting a job with his wife. "What was she before she hooked up with Carolina, a tap instructor?"

Lucius was troubled by possible improprieties on the women's overnight trips. He'd have his aides find out if they'd slept in the same room. And then he'd fret about those teenage boys who'd written C.C. fan letters asking if she could be their substitute teacher. He was irritable when she presented an award to the state high school football champions. Tough as Lucius was, he had been too small to make his high school football team, and he still carried a chip on his shoulder.

The governor decided to "put a lid on this nonsense" by making State Trooper Boo Johnson, head of the troopers' Six-Footers Club, Carolina's escort, and putting Bless Your Heart back in the executive office to file and answer the phone. If anybody gave him a hard time about taking a state trooper off his beat to accompany his wife, he had a ready defense: "You never know when some roughneck Republican might try to get his or her hands on a dainty Democrat like Carolina."

Trooper Johnson went everywhere with C.C., who did not care for his company. She complained to Lucius about "this sorry excuse for a man, this brick wall, standing in my way wherever I go." The trooper wasn't a good conversationalist. It seemed just about all he could say was "Sir," "Ma'am," "Yes," and "No."

In the family Christmas card, there was the Cheshire family—little Mary Lynn, Justice, and Timmy; the governor and his parents, Loyal and Furina—and Trooper Johnson, with what seemed to be a fancy sprig of hair sticking out at the side of his ten-gallon hat. It was hard to tell if Boo was taking on a more feminine look to appease the "militant feminists" who wanted to see more female state troopers on the job. But on closer look, a recipient of one of the Christmas cards noticed a pretty pair of high-heeled shoes visible between Boo's legs and said, "That ain't no hat decoration, that's our dear C.C.!"

At one point C.C. lost Boo by ducking into the ladies' room at the Tennessee–North Carolina visitors' center, right at the state line, and hitchhiking to her parents' house in Memphis, vowing never to return to North Carolina.

But the governor, as usual, smooth-talked her. "Sweet potato pie, I'm sorry. I just wanted to have this fella at your side so's you wouldn't get hurt."

"The only way I'm going to get hurt is when I start hitchhiking everywhere." The governor pictured front-page photographs of C.C. holding out her thumb on a highway, then getting on the back of some low-life thug's motorcycle. The headline would say "C.C. and Company," after the Joe Namath/Ann-Margret movie.

WHEN the United States Senate campaign started, Lucius decided he ought to get tougher on crime by cracking down on drunk drivers. He was for a bill that would give prison terms to waitresses who served the intoxicated driver one too many liquor drinks.

But Virgil Jenkins, who got drunk as a skunk at the only bar in Raleigh open mornings, had—after five shots of Jack Daniel's—plowed into a schoolyard, destroying a jungle gym and the broad-jump sand pit. Worse, he broke the collarbone of a hooky-playing student, twelve, who was smoking in the nearby shrubs. "Imagine what it would have been like had it been at recess," editorials pondered.

Yet when his trial came, a month later, Virgil Jenkins got off as pretty as you please; the arresting officer wasn't present in court.

And where was he? Why, at an Indian crafts festival in Cherokee County, escorting C.C. Cheshire.

"I'm done for," the governor told his staff, "and at my own doing. A goddamned arts-and-crafts festival, when he should have been in the goddamned courthouse." Lucius thought he might even have to withdraw from the campaign.

The press cornered C.C. at the House of Ruth, a shelter for troubled women down on their luck. Some TV reporter with a QT tan and steel-wool hair stuck his microphone in her face while she was sympathizing with a senior citizen who was suffering from a bladder condition.

"Miz Cheshire, a drunk felon was set free yesterday because Trooper Johnson was escorting you to a crafts festival. Any comment?"

"Well now, sweetie," she said with a smile, "I don't keep up with all the goings-on of my drivers. But if you want to ask the trooper himself, I'm sure you could get an answer straight from the source. You can't miss him—he's the six-footer with a big old water head."

And just then one of the troubled women reacted badly to all the TV lights and started to have an epileptic fit. C.C. took off her floral-print scarf and gently but firmly placed it deep in the woman's mouth, right in front of the cameras. A minute later the woman was all smiles and said she wanted to fix everybody some breakfast.

Carolina's lifesaving act was on the six-o'clock local news. It seemed everybody had forgotten about the trooper, who was put back on the highway patrol the next day.

Andy saw C.C. on the six-o'clock news. She was every bit as beautiful as her picture in the newspaper, and charming and graceful besides. He wrote to her, c/o the Governor's Mansion:

Dear Ms. Cheshire,

I made a B minus on my French project by following your recipe for Chocolate Mousse à la Carolina and wanted to thank you. I usually make C's. I also saw you save a life on the television. I wish you had been in our school when Jack Pehoe had his seizure. Most everybody laughed and he nearly passed away. I hear the Smithsonian in Washington, D.C. is planning an exhibit of first ladies dresses. I hope one day your dress will be there. You are prettier than all of them combined.

From,
Andy.

A week later Andy got a note from the Governor's Mansion in a small, invitation kind of envelope. His Adam's apple twitched. It was from *Lucius*.

Carolina and I appreciate your strong show of support for my Senate campaign. We will be in Charlotte soon and hope to have the pleasure of meeting you on a future trip. Best wishes to you and your fine family.

Andy could tell the letter was mass-produced and that the "Charlotte" was typed in to make it seem personal.

ANN MARGRET CHISHOLM lived two doors away from Andy with her mother, the widow Chisholm. Ann Margret was taking time off from college to save up some money and console her mother, who was sad because of the recent death of her husband, Old Man Chisholm.

The man who embalmed Old Man Chisholm took a liking to Ann Margret and used his connections to help get her a job as obituary clerk at the *Observer*. Funeral homes would call her with the names of people who had died and she would type them into her computer terminal. These dead people were categorized not by age or achievement, but by funeral parlor. McGavin, Nightingale, Mercy, and so forth. One time when he was real depressed Andy mastered inscribing the slogan that was ornately printed on all the Nightingale hearses and sales brochures: "Your corpse is our concern."

Ann Margret was not like the other girls in Charlotte. She had short brown hair that was not whirled. She wore loose, baggy dresses and ballet slippers, not earth shoes or Topsiders or cowboy boots. She wore very little makeup, only red lipstick, and sometimes she wore white socks with black pumps. She had seen Andy's letter to the editor about a handwriting contest for adolescents and realized it was from the boy with the bad complexion two houses down who was always checking his mailbox. She made a point of introducing herself when she got one of his packages accidentally, and they became friends.

Andy told Ann Margret about his feelings for Carolina and showed her the fake letter he got back from Lucius after he had written *her*. Ann Margret said not to take it personal, it was just like the governor to open his wife's mail and write a fake note like that. She said Old Man Chisholm, when he was alive, had written to the governor requesting capital punishment for misdemeanors after some boys had burned down his backyard toolshed. All he got back was a letter thanking him for his concern about *forest fires* and a map of the North Carolina wilderness with a picture of Lucius on it.

Andy remembered the toolshed blaze, and he knew who had done it—some tough neighbor boys who wore tank tops to show they had hair under their arms before anyone else. They threatened to beat up people's fathers. Old Man Chisholm had complained about the noise their minibikes made and they had gotten their revenge. The toolshed had Old Man Chisholm's collection of North Carolina license plates in it, from all the way back to "when roads weren't even paved."

The day after the blaze Andy left some oily rags by his father's toolshed and hoped the boys would choose to burn it next. Just a few years before, he had been leaving out milk and fudge for Santa Claus. But the boys had nothing against Andy's father; he had never made a complaint against them. Eventually a neighborhood cat took one of the oily rags in her mouth, as if it had been a kitten, and dropped it by the back door.

"You're not the only one who wants to meet C.C. Cheshire," Ann Margret said. "There's this woman in Pineville who lives right behind the fish market. She's got this big sign that says 'Governor Cheshire, let my husband go. Thirty years is enough for an innocent man.' She calls us over at the paper all the time, trying to get somebody to do a story on her and that sign. But no governor's had the guts to pardon the man."

"What did her husband do?"

"Shot and killed a state trooper, by accident."

"After all *she's* been through, C.C. probably wouldn't object to that," Andy said.

"Yeah, maybe we can hook the two of them up," said Ann Margret.

On Valentine's Day, Andy went to the mailbox hoping to find something from C.C. He'd sent her a Valentine. Andy had never waited for a Valentine before.

"What do you expect?" Andy's mother said. "She doesn't know you. What is it you want from her, anyway?"

"I don't know, it would just be nice to hear from her."

"What are you? Some kind of groupie?"

"No! Maybe she can get me a job in politics someday."

"I'm sure she's got plenty of hangers-on with the same

idea, except they've been hanging on to her for years."

Andy went two houses up to see Ann Margret. A bunch of bouquets were in her living room. A lot of the morticians' sons were courting her, trying to get on her good side so their fathers' parlors might get better placement on the obituary page, or at least an occasional deadline extension.

The morticians couldn't offer themselves to Ann Margret, so they offered their heirs—their sons—many of whom were fine-looking college boys. Mortician McGavin's son Jimmy was a beautiful blond boy who played basketball at Appalachian State and, judging from the size of the bouquets he sent Ann Margret, liked her a lot.

Even though she got flowers, Ann Margret was kind of depressed on Valentine's Day too. Her favorite boy was away at school. And she was afraid that some of the bouquets were from dead people's graves. "I swear I see dirt on the bottom of these petunias, don't you?"

Once the widow Chisholm had gone to bed, Ann Margret offered Andy some red wine in a wineglass and put on some classical music. He thought maybe she wanted to kiss him. Instead, she talked about her boyfriend and what a drag it was typing dead people's names into a computer.

"At least you're getting some journalism experience," Andy said.

"Yeah, right."

"Andy, do you have a girlfriend?"

"Um, no."

"Just Carolina, right?"

"Uh-huh."

"You should really check out this lady in Pineville. You'll love her sign. Y'all have a lot in common." She laughed.

The next morning, Andy went into the bathroom. Even without his brown-framed glasses, which were caked with acne cream, he could tell there were huge red festering pimples—"pus bags," his mother called them—over his face, back, neck, and chest. He had trouble opening his mouth to brush his teeth, because he had smeared on so much acne cream the night before that it froze his face. Even after washing he always still smelled like the ointment, so he would put on lots of aftershave, the kind that came in a big green plastic bottle from the Winn-Dixie.

He was about to get into the shower. He made sure the door was securely locked. He had been in for only a few seconds when he heard a banging sound. Rusty pipes? No, it was somebody banging against the door. Was water leaking through the ceiling downstairs?

Andy opened the door a crack, dripping with water, pus, and blood. One of his pus bags had burst when he brushed against it too hard with the anti-acne soap.

"What are you doing in there?" his father asked.

"What do you think?"

"Your mother is very upset with you."

Why? Had he bleached out the carpet again with his pimple cream? Gotten some of it on her clothes in the wash?

Andy's mother had been furious the time their black cat Frisky lost its hair after he'd kissed it with the cream still on his face. He tried to hide the bald patch with some shoe polish. But the creature licked off the Kiwi and died, discolored and poisoned.

"You didn't give her a Valentine yesterday," his father said.

"What? She didn't give *me* a Valentine yesterday. So what?"

"She had some chocolate for you but threw it out when she realized you didn't have anything for her."

"Oh, Christ."

"You're spending too much time in there," his father said. "I ought to pull you out myself next time."

"Okay, okay, okay."

Andy toweled off and quickly put on all of his clothes. It was too risky to go from one room to another without their protection. His favorite image was of a boy coming from a shower with nothing but a towel around his waist. Oh, well.

Andy couldn't tell his mother he'd forgotten it was Valentine's Day—he'd already complained about not getting a card from Carolina. He couldn't sneak over to Ann Margret's and get some mortician's flowers; she'd probably see him.

He would just apologize to his mother, then go to the mall and get some flowers. They'd be on special, a little wilted.

Andy's mother was down in the kitchen. Her eyebrows were arched up real high, her wig was on crooked, and she was wearing sunglasses—sure signs that she was upset.

"Where's my goddamned vitamin E?" she said. "Have you been putting that on your face too?"

Andy had been using some of her vitamins for his skin; the health magazine had said they were good for acne. He'd even tried applying sugar to his face, mixed with soap. "It's the reverse effect," the article had said. "Taking sugar internally exacerbates acne, whereas applying it externally reverses the process, healing the sores."

"You're such a pig, you know I need them, you selfish pig."

Andy couldn't apologize to her for what she was really upset about. She had told him once, years before, that there were certain "family secrets" that were never to be spoken. Andy knew this was one of them.

Andy swallowed a vitamin and some warm orange juice

left out from the night before; that was his breakfast. Having anything else just made it harder to hold it in all day.

"Bye, Mother."

He started the bomb. It was so cold the car wouldn't go.

Andy's mother came outside without a coat and banged on the windows, screaming. She looked like a reflection in a fun-house mirror. She was so angry, the window was so icy. Her face was pressed against the side window. Andy didn't realize she had so many wrinkles. She had bags of her own, too, under her eyes.

Finally, after the tenth try, the bomb started and Andy put it in reverse.

She was standing right behind it and seemed to be inhaling the exhaust fumes.

"Come on, run me over," she screamed. "Come on, asshole."

What would the neighbors think? He hoped Ann Margret was seeing this.

He finally pulled out and she jumped out of the way. She gave him the finger as he drove off to school.

The car stalled just as he was turning on to Quail Hollow Road. He hadn't let it warm up enough. Something hit him from behind. It didn't hurt; it was just like bumper cars at the amusement park.

Andy got out of his car, looked at the rear and the other car's front. No damage. He walked to the other car, a Pinto. The window rolled down. "Eww grooooss," said a nasaly female voice. It was Terri, the whirly-haired lip-gloss queen.

"Why did you stop like that?" she asked.

"I'm real sorry, it just stalled. The cold . . ."

"I'm telling Mr. Gimlet. You shouldn't be driving that ugly thing to our school, anyway."

Andy didn't want to go to school that day, anyway.

He pulled into the Winn-Dixie parking lot, put on the radio, and lay down in the backseat. He thought death might be better than the stuff he was going through. He wanted to talk to Ryan.

Andy was half-asleep when there was a knock on the car window.

He wasn't sure where he was, but then he saw the Winn-Dixie uniform and recognized the assistant manager. There was a huge color photo of him in the store under an "Employee of the Month" banner. The guy was homely, and Andy thought it was stupid for him to have such a big picture. The guy looked proud, though, holding his certificate.

"No loitering, buddy," he said. But Andy could tell he didn't mean the "buddy" part; he would have called Andy something meaner if he hadn't been in uniform.

What does he care, Andy thought. There are six hundred empty parking spaces. The car started on the ninth try. The assistant manager watched, his arms crossed on his chest, until Andy drove away.

Andy thought it would be safe to drive around Charlotte. His mother had once told him that truant officers these days preferred to work in their comfortable offices in the Education Center downtown, unlike the old hands who patrolled the streets, looking for truants in fast-food franchises and pool halls.

Andy got on South Boulevard and drove past auto-part stores, discount shoe stores, home-furnishings stores, electronics warehouses. He went by the Skate Palace, where a lot of teenagers went but he could never see himself, and just about every fast-food restaurant in existence. The Pizza Hut reminded him of Ryan, the pepperoni-to-go they had eaten together.

There was a new franchise that caught Andy's eye, Arthur Treacher's Fish and Chips. It was green and yellow and had a long hand-painted banner in the window, unusual for a chain; the signs were almost always factory-made. The banner was so long and the writing so small that nobody could read it just driving by, so Andy pulled into the parking lot: "Let Us Hook You on Our New Fish Sandwich. You Bring the Bait and We'll Catch You a Fresh Fish Filet Sandwich and Chips." But Andy knew you couldn't find a worm on such a freezing-cold day.

He remembered that when he was younger, children would find worms on the side of the road on warm summer days after a rainshower and cut them in half with their sandbox shovels. "It don't matter, grows back anyway."

He could probably get some worms from the biology teacher at school, but they would smell like formaldehyde. Besides, the teacher wouldn't want to do Andy a favor. He'd gotten a D first semester, skipping all the classes that dealt with the reproductive system of mammals.

Forget about the worms, Andy said to himself. He was hungry—just pay cash. There was a guy with a green-and-yellow uniform behind the counter. "Top of the day, mate," he said with a British accent.

This was one of those theme restaurants.

Andy ordered a fish filet sandwich, chips, and a Coke. "How 'bout a lemon pie for dessert?" asked the boy. "Pardon?"

"You wouldn't want to get scurvy now, wouldya?"

"No, I guess not."

"Five pounds, four pence, I mean four forty-five."

Andy sat down at one of the salmon-colored vinyl booths. It was still early for lunch, so he had the whole place to himself.

There were pictures of Big Ben and the royal family all over the walls, and slogans like "Stow Yer Trays or Swab the Deck!" Life preservers hung by the "Skippers' " room.

Since this was the grand opening, a queen-size water bed, to be given away in a drawing, was on display. It had a cardboard cutout of the Queen Mother on it. You had to leap over it to get to the condiments stand.

The bed looked pretty inviting, and Andy figured with his mother so mad at him he should probably stay clear of her for a while. He thought of calling Ryan or Ann Margret, but his mother might call them if she wanted to track him down.

Why not just stay here? Andy had read an article in a magazine about a boy who lived in a Burger King and elderly people on fixed incomes who stayed at the all-night Dunkin' Donuts once it started serving hot soup.

Andy asked the manager, Mr. DeLaBounta, "Captain," as he called himself, if he could "dock" for a while; he'd do whatever he could.

Andy knew he wasn't handsome enough to serve the customers. When he once applied for a job at the Chick-Fil-A in the mall, the manager turned him down; he was "a walking advertisement against french fries."

Mr. DeLaBounta said if he patrolled the parking lot at night and made sure the young people from the Pizza Hut next door didn't try to deface the building or break in and bust the water bed with broken beer bottles, he was welcome to stay. It would be a midnight-to-sunrise job, and he'd have to wear a uniform and a bobby's hat and carry a plastic nightstick.

Andy got back into the bomb for some sleep. He thought maybe Ryan would notice he wasn't in school; his mother might miss him when she got home from work, something might happen.

That night Andy put on his Arthur Treacher's patrol uniform: a green-and-yellow polyester shirt, high-water bell-bottoms, and the bobby's hat. He looked in the mirror and knew this couldn't last long.

He walked briskly around the parking lot, hoping nobody would see him, and took off the bobby's hat when Mr. DeLaBounta left for the night. It was Friday, and through the window Andy could see a lot of his schoolmates at the Pizza Hut, having pitchers of beer with their pizzas. Basically, the Pizza Hut was reserved for popular, athletic people. Unpopular people had to get pizza to go and beer from the convenience store. They'd done away with the salad bar at the Pizza Hut after an unpopular girl lost her eye when somebody threw an olive at her head. She now had to wear an eyepatch for the rest of her life and had a stutter to begin with.

Mr. DeLaBounta said he hoped to attract the people who had stuff thrown at them at Pizza Hut. He thought about giving discounts to band members and drama club people. And the book club, too.

Mr. DeLaBounta told Andy that it would be okay to rest on the water bed between surveillance patrols, but "don't get any ideas." It was nice for somebody to think about Andy in that way. The water bed looked inviting, but Andy was afraid his ointment would discolor it—or worse, put a hole in it and cause a flood.

When the morning crew came in ("Mornin', matey, time to catch some fish"), Andy wanted to go home. He wrote a note to his mother on an Arthur Treacher's napkin:

Dear Mother,
I am sorry about forgetting you on Valentine's Day.

No, he couldn't write that.

Instead, he went to the mall and bought two bouquets of flowers from an effeminate man. His mother hated that guy. She had said, "I'd rather have you crippled than like that." On a little note card Andy printed in tiny letters:

Dear Mother,
   I am sorry I was so selfish. I realize you work hard and need those vitamins for energy more than I need them for my pimples. I promise not to do it again. I hope you'll accept this apology.
   Love,
   Andy.

His mother read the note, put the flowers in a vase on the kitchen table, and said to him, "We're friends again."

ANDY thought English class would be the best way to show off his penmanship skills. But Mrs. Bowell, the teacher, hardly ever assigned papers; she preferred three-dimensional projects or skits. You could tell Mrs. Bowell didn't like teaching English that much. She was the drama coach, too, and sometimes got parts at the Pineville Dinner Theater. She said, "Drama is my life's work," and she didn't want to "lug a bunch of papers around."

Mrs. Bowell assigned Mark Twain's *Huckleberry Finn* for the class to read. Everyone was to "utilize the book in a way that promotes racial harmony, in a three-dimensional manner." That meant making something.

Andy thought the best way to have racial harmony was maybe for the two races to eat together. There were a lot of black people in his school, but they ate in one cafeteria, the whites in another. Andy wondered why they built two separate cafeterias to begin with. There was one white girl, named Laskaro, who ate in the black cafeteria, but she didn't count, as she was from overseas.

Andy got to use one of C.C.'s recipes again, Carolina's Cheese Logs. "They're like Lincoln Logs," she had said in the article. "Except they're from North Carolina, not Illinois, and edible." The recipe called for Velveeta, or any processed cheese, to be shaped into a log and rolled in bread crumbs, deep-fried, "and . . . enjoyed!" Andy figured the Lincoln comparison was intended to make the governor seem more statesmanlike.

Andy fixed the logs, froze them, and tied them together with string to make a raft. He took two of his plaster presidents, colored Millard Fillmore's face with a black Magic Marker and labeled him "Jim." Then he made a hat from a thimble and straw for Lyndon Baines Johnson, whom he labeled "Huck." He glued Jim and Huck to the cheese raft.

Maybe blacks and whites, Andy told the class, like Jim and Huck, could eat in the same place together. The cheese raft symbolized the school cafeteria, with Huck representing white students and Jim black students.

Mrs. Bowell seemed to like the project until she took a bite of the cheese raft and had to run out of the room. She threw up in front of a biology class that was meeting outside to study chlorophyll in plants. Evidently she had eaten some of the rubber cement.

Andy got a D for the project but won, for the first time, the approval of the meaner, more popular students. One hunky football player said, "Way to go, dude," as L. Nesbitt, the janitor—or sanitation engineer, as he preferred to be called—was spraying down Mrs. Bowell's throw-up, shaking his head.

SOMETIMES Andy would see Ryan at school, but he never followed him around. There were usually a couple of girls hanging around Ryan, and Andy didn't want to risk making him less popular by associating with him at school. At lunch he didn't even think of sitting next to Ryan in the cafeteria. Instead, he did what all the other unwelcome students did, he went to the library. He would sit at a wooden table and read the *Making of the President* books by Theodore White. His goal was to read all of them: 1960, 1964, 1968, and 1972.

The librarian, Mrs. Nebukula, seemed to know how important it was for some students to avoid being stuck in the cafeteria at lunchtime. So she made it a "special privilege" to use the library at lunch. Even though there were about twenty tables with room for four to six at each, Mrs. Nebukula said that "lunch hour is quiet hour," and only one student was allowed per table. Plus each student had to get a pass at the beginning of each day. They would be given out on a "first come, first served" basis.

So every morning students with nicknames like "Crisco," "Pig Woman," "Crater Face," "Rat Clone," "Camel Back," and "Beauty Queen" would line up at the library door, hoping they would be one of the chosen. There got to be fewer and fewer passes; Mrs. Nebukula had said, "If a pass is lost, that means there is one less student allowed. These passes are bathed in plastic at the Education Center and cannot be replaced." The funny thing was, none of the rejects thought of banding together and protesting the pass policy. They all walked in different directions, heads bowed, to their first class, trying to think of another place to hide during lunch.

Since Andy's mother worked at the Education Center, she got him a special plastic pass that fooled Mrs. Nebukula. So he got to read all of the *Making of the President* books and realized what little he had in common with these men. They were all student council president types, rich or athletic—something he wasn't. Andy read in a history book that Joseph Stalin had bad skin from the chickenpox, but that didn't count since there were no popular elections in the Soviet Union.

Andy thought more and more about First Ladies, and about Carolina Cheshire.

Even though Andy's mother had forgiven him about Valentine's Day, things were still uptight at home because he hadn't been accepted by a fine university. She said he was going to end up spending his life on an assembly line at the Lance snack-food factory if he didn't hear some good news soon.

Andy's grades weren't good, but he tried to explain to his mother how it wasn't his fault entirely. "I didn't know Mrs. Bowell was going to throw up over my project." His mother said that he had a point there, but that was only one example, and the exception rather than the rule.

Andy started going over to Ryan's after school. The rules he made for himself were: (1) Don't bug him at school; and (2) Don't look in a mirror with him. Andy couldn't stop looking at Ryan, though, and wondered if he noticed.

Andy told Ryan about his mother and Valentine's Day. "That's pretty fucked up," Ryan said. Ryan's mother never gave him much trouble and spent most of her time watching TV or making food in the kitchen. Whenever Andy complained about the food at home, his mother would say, "Would you rather have an idiot for a mother, a broad who slaves away in the kitchen all day? Lincoln freed the slaves in 1863!"

Andy's mother was referring to ladies like Ryan's mother. She once told the story of this woman she knew, Fern, who would stand in the kitchen while her family ate dinner in the dining room. While they were eating the main course, she would be making a fancy dessert, and while they ate the dessert, she'd be washing the dishes.

When they had finished dessert, she'd wash those dishes, then sit down and eat the leftovers.

"Is that what you want?" Andy's mother asked him.

"I guess not."

RYAN had been accepted into the University of North Carolina at Chapel Hill and asked Andy if he wanted to be his roommate.

"I haven't been accepted yet. I don't want to hold you up."

One of the guys on the football team had asked Ryan if he wanted to be roommates, but Ryan told Andy, "He's a dickhead. I'd rather just room with you or get a stranger."

"Oh, great."

"This is what our room will look like," Ryan said, and showed Andy a picture from the college edition of *Rolling Stone*. There were beer cans, Coke bottles, a ripped orange La-Z-Boy chair, pizza on the floor, a marijuana plant, a Blondie poster, a stereo, and a TV. "Don't worry, Andy. You can put up some of your Carter stuff."

Andy couldn't imagine even being in that room, but it was great that Ryan could picture the two of them in it, even though he had to see a photo first.

Andy had never prayed, but now he asked God to get him into the university. It was all he wanted.

5

ANDY had only once or twice driven through Pineville, where the lady with the sign in front of her house that said "Governor Cheshire, Let My Husband Go. 30 Years Is Enough for an Innocent Man" lived.

In Pineville haircuts cost $2.50, not $7, and a lot more men wore crew cuts. And there were no tanning booths in the beauty shops, unlike in Charlotte. You could tell where Charlotte ended and Pineville began, even though they shared a road or two. When you got into Pineville, the chain restaurants turned into independent ones. They had names like "Mammy's Kitchen" and "Santa Maria." Instead of 7-Elevens or even a Piggly Wiggly, the convenience store was called The Pineville Fish Market. In addition to junk food, it sold livestock supplies, bait, and fish. It smelled like dead fish instead of spilled lemon-lime slushes.

The lady with the sign was named Dottie Bridges, and she lived right behind the fish market in a neatly kept little white house with green trim. A lot of the other houses behind the fish market had peeling paint and no shingles or aluminum siding. Maybe because they were all behind the fish market and the citizens living there figured nobody would be driving by—unlike Dottie Bridges, who was trying to attract the governor. The script on Dottie's sign was thick, a black Magic Marker job. Not bad, Andy thought, but I could do better.

Andy couldn't get up the nerve to ring the lady's doorbell. What would he say? He went back to the fish market to buy some gas even though he really didn't need any. He usually paid ten cents a gallon extra to have a man do it for him, but at the fish market it was self-service only. He couldn't figure out how to get the nozzle in the tank and was too embarrassed to ask for his money back.

Finally he knocked on Mrs. Bridges's door. A female voice said what sounded like, "Let me stick my finger out the door and see who it is."

"What now?" Andy said.

"Who is it?" said the voice.

"Andy. Ann Margret from the paper suggested I come by."

She opened the door and gently put out her hand. "*I'm* Mrs. Bridges."

Dottie was about fifty years old but still looked good in a red tube top. She had big boobs. Her hair was white and perfectly groomed, the shape of Andy's mother's wig. Dottie was like a southern belle from the past who had kept well. The Charlotte ladies would expect a woman her age to dress like them, in floral-print dresses. Andy remembered his mother had once said that any woman named Dot was probably a harlot, but he wasn't sure if this included women named Dottie, which seemed more down-home than hookerish.

Dottie looked Andy up and down. She didn't seem to disapprove.

"Have you come to write a story about my sign? Two governors have come and gone since the last one y'all did."

"No, ma'am," Andy said. "I'm not with the paper; I just came to talk to you about the governor. I may know a way to get through to him."

"Well, come on in."

Dottie sat Andy down in a comfortable old stuffed chair.

"Can I get you some tea?"

"No, ma'am. Thank you, though."

There were black-and-white pictures of a real big, handsome guy everywhere you looked. That must be her husband, Andy thought. There were also photos of To-kyo Rose and Richard Nixon, matted and framed with headlines announcing their pardons.

Dottie noticed Andy staring at them. "I figure if these two, a traitor and a sorry, dishonest jackass, can get pardoned, my innocent husband can."

"Do you mind if I ask, did your husband really kill a state trooper?"

"Yes, he did. It was an accident, though. But never mind that. Are you kin to the Cheshires? Why do you care about all this?"

"I've been fancying Miz Cheshire ever since I saw some pictures of her sharing recipes, and then I saw her save that woman's life on the TV."

"Are you talking about those cheese logs? They were awful. I've become so cynical, I just don't trust any of these political types. And you know what else? That woman having a seizure was probably just one of the governor's volunteers, pretending."

Andy had never thought of that.

He had brought the letters he'd gotten from famous people, the picture of him and Preston with Jimmy Carter, the *Observer* clipping with Gerald Ford. They were in a photo album marked "Family Pictures."

"Is your daddy in the Secret Service?"

"No ma'am, I just write good letters."

"Honey," Dottie said, "I write to these type people every month and only get mimeographed letters back—if I'm lucky. Nobody wants to mess with my husband's case, especially in an election year. Why, Lucius would send his mama to prison for jaywalking before he'd let somebody call him a New York liberal."

"Is there anything else to try besides politicians?"

"Lord, I've tried everything. It's like pitching pennies in the good-luck well at the mall. You know that preacher who heals people on television? The deaf and so on? Well, Jo Ann Lipscomb, three houses down, said that man cured her mama's cataracts and now she sees clear as day. So I went to his sermon at the coliseum, and you know what? His people wouldn't even let me get onstage, wouldn't let me get near him. They said my problem had to be something physical, so the flock could see a miracle on TV. I felt like such a fool.

"I am on the horns of a dilemma," Dottie Bridges said. She wasn't lying, either.

Governor Cheshire's opponent in the Senate race was the incumbent, Hainus Rainwater, known as the meanest man in the Senate. His biggest concerns were "standing tall" for increased military spending and "fighting to my last breath so-called gay rights" and labor unions. He wore a hat wherever he went. His "little granddaughter" was deaf, so he learned the sign language for "I love you" and used it in public a lot to soften his image some. "Handicapped love, that ought to shut them up," his campaign manager said. Senator Rainwater wouldn't actually have to say the words out loud, though.

Senator Rainwater accused Governor Cheshire of pandering to "liberals, labor unions, and the limp-wristers—you all know what I mean," and of being soft on crime and promiscuity. He made his wife go on a TV commercial and say, "Little schoolchildren are more promiscuous and tardy than ever because of Mr. Cheshire's sorry sex education classes."

One of Hainus's friends owned a local paper in Fuquay-Varina and accused Lucius of being gay outright. In his "Have You Heard?" column, under the headline "Does the Governor Have Something to Hide?" Pou Gill wrote: "Lucius Cheshire has the prettiest little manicured fingernails you ever did see. He flitzes around making chitchat with the ladies. In the Marines we had names like Sadie and Bessie for men who walk the way he does. A gunnery sergeant would take the sway out of his butt in twenty-four hours. We want and need a man who walks and talks like a real man to represent North Carolina in the United States Senate. A man like Hainus Rainwater."

This was the atmosphere Dottie and Andy had to try to free a convicted felon in.

"We've got to focus on C.C., not Lucius," Andy told Dottie. "She probably doesn't like state troopers after all that trouble she went through. She'd be the one to convince Lucius, if anybody can."

"Can't hurt," Dottie said. "Andy, I've got to go to work. Come by there in a couple days and I'll get you some lunch and we'll talk more about this."

Dottie worked as a waitress at the Santa Maria.

"Now, I appreciate your help, but I'm still not sure I understand why you're interested . . ."

"I just want to hook up with a First Lady."

"She's a married woman, darlin'."

"Oh no, not *that* way," Andy said. "It would just be fun to meet her with a purpose."

"Uh-huh. Well, I've got to go."

Andy was driving around Pineville just after leaving Dottie when he saw it. A president's birthplace. All these years he'd lived in Charlotte and didn't realize a presidential log cabin was just a few miles away, in Pineville. There was a sign on the huge green lawn that said: "James K. Polk Memorial. Industrious President of Nineteenth-Century United States."

There were free guided tours. Andy tagged along on the back of one with a bunch of elementary school students. The tour guide was an older woman, very proper. She was showing the children a barn that was similar to the one Polk had. There were a pig, a cow, and a horse.

"Young people, don't touch the pig, he bit me once."

"Why's that?" asked a little towhead.

"Just had a notion to, I imagine."

The class wise-acre asked if the cow was really the same one that was there in Polk's day.

"Don't be silly, honey."

Andy was disappointed to hear that the log cabin did not really belong to the Polks. It was just a facsimile. He wanted to touch something Polk had touched. He had to settle for walking the very same pastures.

They got to the Polk museum, where an educational film about the Polk presidency was being shown. The narrator said: "Polk's remarkable achievements may be credited to his personal dedication and sincerity." The annexation of Texas, for example. This gave the tour guide a chance to sit down for a while. But the students had a hard time keeping their minds on the film, and finally their teacher said, "Y'all hush up and listen to the film or you'll have to watch it twice."

Andy went up to the Polk museum lady and wiped his hands on his pants to make sure they weren't greasy or sweaty in case she'd want to shake. It was dark, the only light there was from the Polk film. The lady's name was Vivian Mariette. She had been a tour guide there for twenty years. She said it was an easy job.

"Not many people care to find out about their heritage, so all we get are these student tours. It's not bad, but sometimes it gets right lonely. Every now and again Miz Berryhill comes by and hands out the brochures"—she pointed to a stack of pamphlets by the entrance—"but she keeps to herself. She is elderly, you know, and doesn't have that much to say. But the benefits are good, being state employees and all."

"Yes ma'am," Andy said. "Do any state officials ever come by to say hey?"

"No, huh-uh, they sure don't. We get the mayor sometimes, but that's about it. The state auditor came by once, about five years ago, and asked if we couldn't cut back on the livestock, so we just kept one of each animal as you saw. Every now and again the high school students come by, they like to neck during the film presentation. I don't know why they come here, maybe they can't afford to see the popular movies. It *is* awful expensive, with the popcorn and Co'-Colas—"

Andy interrupted. "Ma'am, have you ever thought of inviting the governor's wife, Carolina?"

"Good heavens. Now, why on earth would she come?"

"It's a campaign year and she's got to get out and meet a lot of people."

"Are you with the campaign, young man?"

"No ma'am, I just think it would be great to see her in Pineville."

"Come to think of it, we *will* be having a ceremony next month, which Miz Cheshire might enjoy. One of Miz Polk's dresses will be coming up from Nashville. We're going to put it on display here before it goes to the Smithsonian."

"Why not invite Mrs. Cheshire?"

"Well, you know, I will."

"And if you could introduce me to her when she comes, I'd sure appreciate it."

"You bet I will."

Andy was the happiest he'd been in a long time. Now he could be formally introduced to the First Lady of North Carolina without looking like just some kind of hanger-on. Maybe he could help this Dottie Bridges lady, too.

Andy went to the Santa Maria. It was lunch hour, so most all the tables were full. Andy found an empty one by the men's room. He saw Dottie in action, waiting on a lot of older businessmen with potbellies and clots of hair combed over their bald heads. A lot of them wore ties that didn't even come close to their bellies.

"What'll you have, handsome?" Dottie said to one of the men, who wasn't.

"How 'bout you in a dish?" he said.

"Lord, I don't believe there's one big enough for all of me," said Dottie.

"I've got something big for ya," said the man, and all the fellows at the table started laughing as he pointed to his groin area.

"Are you talking about your truss, sugar?" All the men laughed even louder, except for the man with the truss.

Dottie called all the men she waited on "handsome." Andy saw why these guys liked her so much, and why she wore a tube top. She wasn't as sexy as those high school waitresses, but she still looked good. Besides, those high school girls were so stuck on themselves they wouldn't remember the customers' orders, let alone sweet talk them.

Dottie came to Andy's table. "Hey, darlin', what are you doing back so quick?"

"We're going to meet Carolina!"

Dottie said hold on, they could talk after the lunch hour settled down. "Can I get you something to eat? It's on the house."

"I'll have the manicotti and some garlic bread."

The pasta was soggy and the sauce was from a jar. The garlic bread was just a toasted hamburger bun, probably Wonder, with margarine and garlic salt. The men must come here just for the atmosphere and Dottie, Andy thought. And the prices were reasonable.

"Can I get y'all some pie for dessert? It's real good!"

"Get me a piece of that walnut pie, Dottie."

"How about a scoop of ice cream to go with that?"

The owner gave Dottie twenty cents for each piece of pie she sold by making the suggestion, a nickel for each scoop of ice cream.

When lunch was over, Dottie sat next to Andy. It took her a while to get her tips out of her jean pockets; they were pretty tight.

"Not bad," she said after counting it up.

Andy told her how the Polk's birthplace lady was going to try to have Carolina over. This would be a fine way for them all to be formally introduced; they wouldn't look like a couple of nuts.

"Shoot, why didn't I think of that?"

Andy suggested they get started right away. They should work on a letter to give to Carolina when they met her.

"I wish we had some Polk stationery to write on, but we'll make do," Andy said.

Dottie talked, Andy wrote and revised. The letter would be from Dottie. It went:

Dear Mrs. Cheshire,

We are certainly proud to have had a president living in our town, and your visiting us makes our pride shine all the more.

80

I would like a moment of your time to discuss a matter that weighs on my heart. I realize you are a very busy woman, but if you could give this matter some attention, I would be eternally grateful.

My husband, Walter Bridges, Jr., has been incarcerated in the Mecklenburg County Prison for some thirty years now. He was convicted of murdering a state trooper, though it was unintentional, and in self-defense.

It all happened on our honeymoon. We were in Asheville, where we had just been on a tour of the Biltmore Castle and Mansion, and we were having a picnic lunch on the grounds there. My mother, Mrs. Burdette, had fixed us a meal of fried chicken, tomato sandwiches, and pecan pie. Given that this was our honeymoon, one thing led to another and Walter kissed me on the lips. Just at this time, a state trooper came along and started calling me certain names, "easy" being the only one I could even mention in a letter to the First Lady of our state. He said that such goings-on were forbidden on state property and continued to question my moral character.

My husband, who is six feet, six inches in his stocking feet and a veteran (he was a boxer in the armed forces, too), had no choice but to defend my honor. The trooper must have been startled by my husband's presence when he raised up to his full height. The trooper pulled out his revolver. "Put that down and fight like a man," my husband said. I see this just as clear as if it was yesterday, Mrs. Cheshire. Walter looked so handsome and the sky was blue as your name, Carolina. I was very much in love.

Well, somehow in the ruffle that ensued, the gun was fired and the bullet lodged in the trooper, hit with his own gun, his own bullet. My husband did not flee. He calmly instructed me to get help. He tried to revive the man. When other state troopers and Biltmore Castle employees arrived, Walter was handcuffed and punched. The man was dead. "You've killed one of our men," said one trooper.

Since that day some thirty years ago, my husband has been imprisoned and I have remained true to him. I am over fifty now and not much to look at, but I was in my day and have resisted many an overture. I know that you know what love is, Mrs. Cheshire. I have seen many pictures of you and your husband on campaign literature and so forth. I know the governor is a busy man, but if you could somehow call his attention to this matter, I would have reason to live with a glimmer of hope. I know I will see my man in providence, but I would like to spend some time with him on this earth while we still have what is left of our honeymoon virility.

Gratefully,

Dottie Bridges

(Mrs. Walter Bridges, Jr.)

Andy was surprised to find out that this lady in a tube top, who was so familiar with salesmen, had gone so long without ever being spoiled.

As much as Andy wanted to see Walter free, he did not want to set eyes on him. It would ruin his image of him, the one Dottie had in her locket, the pictures she had in her home.

Andy called Vivian Mariette at the Polk Memorial a week later, and she said yes, Carolina would be coming to celebrate the arrival of Mrs. Polk's dress from Tennessee before it went to the Smithsonian. Mrs. Mariette said Carolina liked the idea of Mrs. Polk's dress going from Tennessee to North Carolina to Washington, the very same road she hoped to travel. The Polk people were hoping that the visit would get more people to come to the memorial, as summer break was nearing and school groups wouldn't be coming through.

*   *   *

WHEN Carolina came to Pineville, Andy skipped school
and took Ryan with him. He hadn't taken anybody to a
political event since Preston met Jimmy Carter. Ryan
thought the idea of going to Polk's home was hilarious.

It was so sunny and beautiful that Andy started feeling
sick over how much worse the bright sun would make his
acne look. Then again, a tan might help. The day was so
pretty that the ceremony was going to be held outside.
Carolina was also concerned that an indoor gown ceremony might be seen as too highfalutin. A lot of salesmen
and clerks from Pineville gathered on the grass.

Mrs. Polk's dress was encased in a huge transparent
plastic box. It was displayed on a female dummy donated
by the local department store. The dress was pure white; it
had not yellowed in the least. Andy thought it was a
shame that they had not kept Mrs. Polk as well, maybe in
formaldehyde. Evidently they did that only in communist
countries.

All of the women oohed and aahed over the dress,
saying they hadn't seen anything like it since *Gone With
the Wind*. Some of the men began feeling awkward about
going to a ceremony for a dress, so they started talking
about what a fine-looking woman Carolina was, or how
they would like to play some ball once this ceremony was
over with.

The Pineville choir was there, too. They sang "Dixie,"
"God Bless America," and "Up, Up With People," using
hand motions during the last.

Carolina, now with Bless Your Heart since Trooper
Johnson's removal, came in a sedan, because a convertible
would be too flashy for the campaign. They were only
fifteen minutes late. Carolina was just as pretty as her
picture. Vivian Mariette introduced herself to Carolina,
who put a hand to her boob and mouthed "Oh, my"

when she saw the dress. "Why, isn't that the prettiest thing you ever did see?" she said. Then Vivian Mariette introduced Carolina to the crowd, saying it had been a long time since somebody this important had been to the "Polkstead," and how delighted she was to see "the prettiest First Lady the old North State ever had." Carolina looked straight at her the entire time, with a smile on her lips.

"Damn, it's hot," Andy heard a man named Hoyt say. "I sure hope we're not in for a long speech." You could see a lot of sweat stains when men took off their jackets. People were looking around for napkins or tissues to wipe their brows with. But Carolina appeared to be in a different climate. Her face stayed perfect, almost like a mask.

Ryan had gotten stoned and he stayed in the background, playing with the farm animals and laughing a lot. "Wow, I wonder what pigs think about," he said. Andy wished he'd pay more attention to the ceremony. It was so cool, seeing someone like Carolina in person after seeing her in the media and his mind.

Carolina said she was proud to be part of such a big to-do. "I'm not running for Mrs. Polk's position . . . yet," she said with a big wink, and the crowd chuckled along with her. That was the thing with being a famous person, Andy noticed: Even if you said something that wasn't laugh-out-loud funny, people would laugh out loud, anyway. "But as y'all know, my husband, Lucius, is running for the United States Senate, and we'd appreciate your help."

Afterward the press started asking her questions. Most of them were easy ones, like "How do you find Pineville, ma'am?" and "How would it feel to wear a dress like Mrs. Polk's?" But Brie Quinby from Channel 3 asked "Where's the trooper?" and everything got real quiet.

"Why, I don't know, Brie. Maybe you ought to try nine-one-one," and that was that.

Carolina shook a few more hands while Bless Your Heart discreetly went back to the car and started it. Carolina headed for the car, but Vivian Mariette gently took her elbow, guided her back to the crowd, and said "Miz Cheshire, this is Andy. He's the boy who thought of inviting you down here."

Carolina looked at him and smiled the same smile she gave everyone, no matter what they looked like, and held out her hand to shake. "Is that right?" she said. "I appreciate it." Andy thought it would be better to kiss the hand, maybe make an impression. He knew if he said anything his voice would quiver. But he missed, and kissed a couple of Carolina's fingers instead of the back of her hand.

"Try again, honey," Carolina said, and held up the back of her hand to his lips. She almost made a fist to hide the fingers.

Andy pursed his lips. One kiss. "See, honey, practice makes perfect."

Andy's knees were trembling. "I've, I've followed your recipes," he said.

"Well, isn't that wonderful?" said Carolina. "I hope you're not keeping them from your mama!"

"No ma'am, she doesn't like to cook."

"Is that right?" Carolina smiled and turned to Vivian Mariette. "I've got to run to a pig pickin' in Lincolnton. Thank you so much for having me."

Dottie Bridges elbowed Andy.

"Um, Miz Cheshire?" he said.

"What now, honey?"

For the first time there was a change in Carolina's expression, as if Andy had just thrown everything off balance.

"Miz Cheshire, this is Mrs. Bridges."

"Pleased to meet you," Carolina said.

Dottie put her head down some and shook hands.

She handed her letter to Carolina. Andy had rewritten it the night before in a Declaration of Independence script.

"I'd appreciate your taking a look at this, Mrs. Cheshire."

She took it in a way that would be called gentle if it had been anyone else, but for her it was downright brusque. "I sure will. Bye-bye now!"

Everybody waved.

When Carolina got into her car she waved back.

Andy and Dottie watched Carolina as she was driven away. She wasn't reading the letter.

Andy decided to go to the dermatologist, and Ryan said he'd come along. This was the first time Andy was going to see one. His mother had said there was no need for it, that it was "all the pizzas that you're eating with that boy . . . what's his name? . . ." Andy knew it was more than pizza. Ryan said, "Maybe it's something emotional. You do seem kind of uptight a lot."

Andy called the dermatologist's office to make an appointment, but when the lady who answered asked, "What's your problem?" he hung up. He couldn't say the word "acne." So he called back and said his problem was hemorrhoids.

The receptionist was a mean-looking lady with curly gray hair and a crooked mouth. She spoke out of the side of it.

"Name?"

Andy answered.

"It looks like your problem is acne, not hemorrhoids. Fill out this form."

Andy sat next to Ryan in the waiting room.

"You've got hemorrhoids, too?" Ryan asked. "I thought only retired people got those."

Andy put Ryan's name down for a person to contact in case of emergency. But what could happen? The dermatologist might pop a pimple too hard and break Andy's back?

Andy certainly didn't want his mother to know he was seeing a doctor. She said she hadn't seen one since she gave birth to him. "Nobody's touched me since."

The nurse came in; she looked kinder than the receptionist. The last female to hold his hand had been a nurse, years before, when the orthodontist was installing his braces.

"You've got hemorrhoids"—she looked down on her chart—"Andrew?"

"No ma'am, that's a mistake. I've got . . . pimples. See what happens when you eat too much chocolate and worry about your grades?" The woman forced a laugh. She must really feel sorry for me, Andy thought.

Then the doctor came in. He was the first person in years to see Andy with his shirt off. "Mmmm," he said.

He gave Andy a prescription for pills and ointment.

"Should I keep using any of the stuff I use now? Does it do any good?"

The doctor, very striking in an almost feminine way, rolled his eyes. He motioned to Andy's face, then to his chest. "Obviously not," he said.

"I could inject the inflammations on your back, chest, and neck. That would make them recede."

The thought of having needles in his neck was almost as

bad as the thought of getting more pimples, if that was possible.

"I don't think so, maybe later," Andy said.

"Have it your way," said the nice doctor.

"Forty-five," the receptionist said. She didn't say "dollars."

"I'm five short," Andy said.

"We don't bill. Next time bring the full amount."

"I'm sorry," Andy said.

"When do you want your next appointment"—she looked at his chart—"Acne Vulgaris?"

Evidently it was the office policy to call delinquent patients by the name of their skin condition.

"Two weeks."

FINALLY Andy was accepted into the University of North Carolina at Chapel Hill. He would live with Ryan. He wasn't sure if it was his prayer to God or his extracurricular activities that had made the difference. He had sent the admissions board one of his articles on Jimmy Carter buttons that had appeared in *The Political Accumulator*.

To celebrate, his parents took him to the most expensive restaurant in the mall. They ordered two steak dinners and shared. You could tell it was a classy restaurant because the salad bar had real bacon bits and chunky, not creamy, blue cheese dressing.

Andy wanted to get dessert, but his mother said they could buy a cake at the Winn-Dixie for the price they charged for one slice here, and the cake they served here was from the supermarket, anyway.

Andy's parents asked him who his roommate was going to be.

"What's his name again?"

"What do his parents do?"

"Is he a fast driver?"

"Does he study hard?"

"Ryan." It was the first time Andy said his name in front of them. He blushed when he said it, or at least it felt like he did. But between the dim restaurant lighting and his naturally pimple-red face, he was sure nobody could tell.

"When do we get to meet him?"

"Soon," Andy lied.

Andy's parents told him he should get a job. They'd pay for his tuition at college, but now that he didn't have to worry about his high school grades, he should start saving for spending money.

Arthur Treacher's had folded. The "mateys" were Irish, not English, and did not have green cards.

Andy asked Dottie Bridges for a job at the Santa Maria. He had almost forgotten about her husband but figured he hadn't been pardoned. He would have read about it.

Dottie said no, Carolina hadn't even written back, and no, he could not have a job at the Santa Maria. The owner, Mr. Brady, did not like to hire young people. They always asked for time off: "Hey, Mr. Brady, can I have Friday off, it's the prom," or "Gee, Mr. B., I've got tickets to see the new popular band. Mind if I take off?"

"Well, he wouldn't have any trouble with me, I don't go out."

"Be that as it may," Dottie said. "Have you tried Polk's place?"

"They have trouble getting enough money just to keep the farm animals as it is."

"Well, good luck," she said.

Andy had to go to the mall.

The real popular people sold Levi's; heavyset ones worked at the Cheese Hut; cool people worked at the Record Bar. Borderlines were safe at Eckerd Drugs, working the grill. The places Andy went let him fill out applications, but he could tell they were not about to give him a job. He did not know who to put down for references. Any adult who thought Andy was upstanding collected political buttons and lived out of state. He put down "Dottie Bridges," even though she seemed mad at him.

The only job the mall offered him was in maintenance. The guy said with a wink that Andy would get only minimum wage but got to fish out the coins from the wishing well once the mall closed. "I tell ya," the man said, "it comes to more than you'd think it would."

Andy went to a United Parcel Service call-in. All the job applicants, all guys, had to strip to their underpants and have a physical on the spot. Andy told the UPS man that he had left his car running, with the keys in the ignition, then rushed out and drove away.

He drove to the other side of town and saw a "Help Wanted" sign at one of the Burger Chefs. Everybody there was black. He asked Mr. Houston, the manager, for an application.

Andy filled it out and was ready to leave. But Mr. Houston asked him to sit back down and joined him.

Mr. Houston was wearing an upgraded uniform, part cotton, and he had on a tie. Instead of a four-cornered paper hat, he wore one that was real fabric, with a tassel on it. Mr. Houston had excellent posture, even when he was sitting down.

"May I ask what brought you to this particular franchise?"

Andy didn't want to say that he'd been told at the Chick-Fil-A in the mall that he was a walking advertisement against french fries, or that he couldn't get a job in the rich side of town. "I was driving by." That was good enough.

90

"Have you had any prior experience in the food service field?"

"No sir, but I've always enjoyed cooking."

"The main, uh, prerogative of our establishment is to serve the customer a quality product in an efficient period of time in a friendly manner at a reasonable cost. It is a team here."

"Yes sir."

"When can you start?"

"Now?"

"What is your waist size?"

Mr. Houston went into the back room and brought out a uniform that was even worse than the one at Arthur Treacher's, all polyester, orange and brown.

"Well, now, you certainly are tall, so these particular pants may be small on you. We'll just have to make do. Come in tomorrow at four P.M."

Back home, Andy looked at himself in uniform in the full-length bathroom mirror. He was horrified. The almost plastic-feeling Burger Chef shirt was a V-neck and showed all his acne. He would just have to wear one of his mock turtlenecks underneath. He hoped Mr. Houston wouldn't hold it against him or throw him off the Burger Chef "team." The pants Mr. Houston gave him weren't just high-waters, they were bell-bottoms. But they weren't like ordinary bell-bottoms—their double-knit construction kept them permanently flared. He never knew pants could stretch like that.

The other requirement at Burger Chef was to wear brown shoes, not sneakers. The only shoes Andy had like that were the earth shoes he hadn't worn in years. They were very tight, and Andy wasn't sure the three different shades of brown would fit the regulations.

As soon as Mr. Houston saw him, he did not say "Hello," but, "*What* are you wearing?"

"A turtleneck, actually it's a mock turtleneck."

"Well a *mock tur-tle-neck* is not part of our uniform, and your shoes are a dis-grace."

"But I sort of have a skin condition and my doctor says that I have to keep that area covered, especially in a greasy environment."

"Our product is not greasy. It is charcoal-broiled. And what does that have to do with those sorry-assed shoes?"

Mr. Houston said that Andy would have to get a note from the doctor to permit the turtleneck and that he'd have to get new shoes entirely, unless he had a medical excuse for that, too. Andy thought of his "Podiatrists for Carter" button.

That night, Andy sat in Ryan's room in his Burger Chef uniform. They filled out their dorm-room application for the university. For the first time, he saw their two names together in writing that was not his own.

Andy asked Ryan if he could forge a doctor's note for Andy so he could get this job flipping hamburgers. He *was* going to go to medical school, so it wouldn't be that dishonest. "I really don't want to go back to that dermatologist," Andy said.

"I don't blame you. That receptionist was a real bitch. When I'm a doctor, I'll never hire anybody like that."

Andy thought that by the time Ryan was a doctor and could examine him, his skin would be all cleared up.

He hoped the brown leather shoes he got at the Shoe Town would be enough to pacify Mr. Houston. But he hadn't gotten on the man's good side, and he never realized how much discipline was behind making a hamburger, fries, and a medium Coke. Everything was computerized, timed to the second. Even the batter for the apple-pie crust was premade and sent from corporate headquarters, frozen.

92

"Our burger is a burger: whether you're in Tacoma or Timbucktu, you'll get the same delicious taste," Mr. Houston said.

Andy worked with two girls, La Tonya and Fern. Their nicknames were "Ice Tea" and "Rye Bread." The guy he worked with had "Curtis" on his name tag, but everybody called him "Peanut Butter." Ice Tea was heavyset and Andy recognized her from school, but they had never spoken.

Andy hoped that they would name him after a food item or beverage, but he ended up with "Ugly" and "Goofy Motherfucker."

When he mopped up the floor, the girls laughed and said, "You a mess. You just makin' the floor dirtier, you think you still got your pajamas on." But sometimes he could make them laugh by joking that he was from overseas, and that was why he had so much trouble adjusting. "I would be a prince if only I were in my home country of Lusitania," Andy said with a make-believe accent.

"You a trip," said Ice Tea.

"Where Lusitania at?" said Rye Bread.

"Shut the fuck up or I'll kick your ass," said Peanut Butter.

Andy liked Ice Tea a lot because she smelled like Ryan somehow.

Peanut Butter was the head chef; he'd been working there for three years and had a son. He was friends with Mr. Houston and didn't have much patience for Andy, either. He was irritated when he showed Andy how to flip the burgers. Andy had never noticed black guys before, but Peanut Butter's arms made him get hard sometimes. He had to lean against the hot grill to force it down. Peanut Butter's arms were so well developed that Mr. Houston allowed an infraction of the uniform code by letting him roll up his sleeves three-quarters of an inch. Andy wished it were an infraction to wear pants five inches too high with flared bottoms nine inches too wide.

"It's all in the wrist," Peanut Butter said as he flipped the burgers perfectly with a regulation spatula. Maybe it was some kind of mental block, but Andy always had a hard time using his wrists for anything. His skinny hands used to droop down from his weak wrists when he was in elementary school, and his mother would slap them and say, "No loose bananas."

When Andy put his first burger on the grill, the piece of paper separating the patties stuck to it, smoking up the whole place and messing up the grill. Burgers couldn't be served for over ten minutes, and customers had to either wait or get the fried-fish-filet sandwich instead.

Mr. Houston got angry at Peanut Butter for this fiasco, blaming him for not training Andy properly. It was like the army movies Andy had seen. When one guy had a lump in his bed, all the other guys in his platoon had to do a bunch of sit-ups as punishment.

"Shall I have to take this particular employee under *my* wing?" Mr. Houston glared at Peanut Butter.

Peanut Butter told Andy he would beat the shit out of him unless he quit. During a surprise inspection from corporate headquarters, he once locked Andy in the condiments freezer. All there was to eat were the "fixin's"— lettuce, onions, secret sauce, cinnamon sprinkling for apple pie—so it wasn't like getting a free meal. The wage was hourly, and Andy was on the clock while in the freezer.

Mr. Houston was pretty smooth about the whole thing. Instead of firing Andy outright, he just got his schedule down to a half-hour per week. It took Andy that long just to drive there.

Mr. Houston said he had heard through the fast-food

grapevine that a new restaurant that sold just biscuits was looking for employees, and manual dexterity would not be a prerequisite.

Biscuitville had a big facade, like an old southern mansion. Inside, it had plastic chairs and tables like anywhere else. The big difference was, all they sold were biscuits, so the employees had to pretend it was always morning—morning, noon, and night. The cashier had to say "Good morning. Welcome to Biscuitville" even when it was dark outside. And the biscuits, whether they were stuffed with egg, cheese, ham, sausage, or oleo, all had wrappers that said "Mornin'," just below a smiling sun. The plan was that people could have the meal they probably skipped, or if they had had a bad day could pretend they were starting over.

It was impossible to mess up this job; all Andy had to do was stir up some batter, then pour it in a mold. He had to wear just a Biscuitville T-shirt; his own pants were fine. One guy he worked with and his friend gobbed into the batter every now and then, but Andy didn't want any trouble. He kept his mouth shut and ate the meat and cheese without the biscuit. By the time summer was over, he had saved more than a hundred dollars—spending money for college.

6

A NDY'S mother couldn't get in the car that was taking him to college. She was crying so hard she was afraid she'd get carsick.

"Maybe community college wouldn't be so bad," she said. "You could stay at home and take the bus."

She stood in the driveway, in tears. Now Andy would be alone with his father, confined in the car. It would be the first time they'd be alone together, at least as far as Andy could remember.

His father was interested in what he threw away, so Andy was always careful to rip everything up before he put it in his wastebasket—especially the sheets of paper that said *andyryanandyryanandyryan* in many different shapes. Sometimes he even went into the bathroom and burned the names in the bathtub. And whenever Andy had to use the bathroom, he made sure the door was locked and the drawers pulled out in front of the door for protection. It just seemed the safe thing to do.

Once Andy found his father's high school yearbook in the attic. He wasn't hated; classmates wrote messages to him that began: "To a swell fellow . . ." He looked okay in his yearbook picture, but Andy didn't look that bad in his, either. Evidently everybody's yearbook pimples were always retouched, even before high-fashion photography became popular.

Andy looked at the side of his father's face from the passenger seat. No acne scars. They stopped at an intersection just before getting on the highway to Chapel Hill. Two high school girls in a van were in the next lane. They looked at Andy and grimaced. Did his father notice?

Andy made sure the radio stayed on the entire time, even when bad songs like "The Piña Colada Song" came on.

Andy heard a siren and thought, There's no siren in "The Piña Colada Song," unless this is some new disco version. It wasn't the disco version, they were getting pulled over.

They stopped on the side of the highway, and a state trooper climbed out of his vehicle and slowly walked toward theirs. Big and tall. Could it be Trooper Johnson? No, his name tag said "Holmes."

"Did you know you were going ten miles over the limit?"

Andy's father had to get into the trooper's car. Front seat.

Andy watched them in the rearview mirror. While the trooper was talking into his radio, Andy's father glared at Andy.

When he was back in the driver's seat, his father said, "Add another thousand bucks to your college education."

That's how much his father's car insurance would increase.

Andy thought about telling his father the Trooper Johnson story while they were on the subject, but remembered he didn't like to hear that political stuff. "That's between you and your mother," he had once told Andy.

"God, I'm really sorry, Dad," was all Andy could say.

When they were driving through the rural parts of the state and couldn't pick up a radio station, Andy's father started talking about the radio-wave transmission process, how it worked. It didn't make any sense, but Andy followed each fact about high or low frequency with a "Really?" and another question about it. That way, there wouldn't be silence.

Andy's father opened his mouth and nothing came out. Then he tried again. "I'm sure you'll be meeting plenty of fellows in college."

"Yeah?"

"Why not start a band with them?" his father asked. "I was part of a barbershop quartet with my buddies—way back when."

"What are you talking about? The only instrument I ever even *tried* to play was the recorder."

Andy turned the radio back on, even though there was more static than music.

They were both pretty hungry, but Andy's father did not want to make unnecessary pit stops. Being pulled over by the trooper had already screwed up his designated travel time of two hours, forty-five minutes.

"We'll have to eat when we get there," his father said. In that case, Andy would just as soon eat with Ryan instead.

When they got into Chapel Hill, Andy's father swerved and followed the "Hospital" sign instead of the "University" sign.

"What are you doing?" Andy asked.

"We're going to the hospital."

"What for?" Andy asked. "Are you okay?"

Maybe that ticket and thoughts of raised insurance rates had given him one of those silent strokes.

"Lunchtime," his father said.

It turned out one of the fellows from his father's company had stayed at a hospital in Chapel Hill when he got cancer from smoking too many cigarettes. The guy said the food was aces, and the price was right.

Andy was just relieved that his father wasn't about to keel over.

They got into the hospital through the emergency room entrance and followed arrows on the corridor walls to the cafeteria. There were a lot of people with catheters and on stretchers. Everybody in the cafeteria seemed sad; Andy felt wrong being there. Maybe somebody had just died, a close friend or relative had lost a body part. Here was all this grief, and Andy's father took him there by choice, because the prices were good.

One lady in the cafeteria had a goiter the size of a tennis ball on her neck, but Andy wasn't sure if she was a visitor or a patient. He wanted to ask her if she ate fish.

The food was just like in high school, maybe a little nicer. The cafeteria ladies wore surgical gloves on their hands instead of Baggies. Had they been used before by the doctors?

Andy and his father got roast beef, wax beans, Jell-O salad with hunks of fruit in it and a nondairy topping on it. The plates and utensils were paper and plastic, to avoid contamination.

The meat was so tough and the plates so flimsy that it was impossible to cut it without having the plate slide every which way. Andy thought he'd have to skip the roast beef and have just wax beans and Jell-O for lunch. But Andy's father figured it all out and cut his meat while Andy held the plate, and vice versa.

Andy's eyebrows were arched and he wasn't saying anything. He knew it would be stupid to start a fight about food when he wasn't at home anymore. Then Andy's father started talking without being asked any questions: "When I was your age, I had to work my way through school. Lived at home, worked at the hospital. Times were hard, there wasn't much food at home. I'd be happy to eat hospital leftovers. We were allotted one meal per shift, but me and my buddy Jarvis were big fellows, big appetites. We'd be happy to find a stray tray that hadn't been touched—say, from a fellow or a missus who'd passed away or gone into surgery—save for maybe a finger mark in the tapioca."

Andy now understood why his father had never complained about food at home. It wasn't that bad if you'd eaten off the plates of dead people as a youth.

After listening to this story, Andy wasn't hungry anymore, so he let his father have his Jell-O.

On the way out of the hospital Andy made a mental note to remember where the dermatology department was; he knew he'd be spending a lot of time there.

As soon as they pulled into the parking lot by the dorm, Andy quickly put out his hand to give a good-bye shake to his father. He knew his father wouldn't try to hug or kiss him, but he didn't want to take any chances.

"Oh, no." Andy's father wouldn't shake. "I'll help bring your things up." There wasn't much—turtlenecks, jeans, shoes, a huge Jimmy Carter poster.

"Really," Andy said, "I can handle it."

A cheerful girl in a Carolina-blue shirt that said "Orientation" with a smiley face in the O came to their car. She looked like one of those girls in high school who could be downright cruel, but now that she was in college she was volunteering to be kind and helpful.

"Well, hey, y'all! Welcome to Carolina! Do y'all need some help?"

"No." His father was so brusque that Andy felt bad for the girl.

The building was from the 1950s—tall and straight, a lot of concrete. In the lobby families were standing around, surrounded by their children's weight sets, Smith Corona typewriters, guitars, stereos. They were introducing themselves to other sets of parents, making dinner plans.

I hope Ryan isn't there yet, Andy said to himself.

But when the door to room 910 opened, Ryan was putting his clothes away, and all he had on was a pair of shorts. It was real hot, no air conditioners allowed. This was exactly the way Andy did not want his father to meet Ryan.

Andy introduced them and looked down when they shook hands.

"Well, thanks, Dad, we've got everything."

"Let me look around. Say, where's the bathroom?"

Down the hall. He went.

"Fellows, it works."

"*Really*, thanks a lot, Dad."

"It was a pleasure meeting you, sir," Ryan said as Andy's father shook his hand. Once he was out the door, Ryan said, "He seems nice enough."

Then Andy told Ryan about lunch at the hospital.

CHAPEL HILL was a charming southern university town, like all the brochures said, and James K. Polk had once lived in one of the dorms. Maybe he could live there with Ryan next year, Andy thought. He was hoping that the student body would be kind of bohemian, so he brought a T-shirt that said "Musicians United for Safe Energy." It had a lot of band names listed on it. Andy thought it would be a hit.

But everything seemed more like one big high school pep rally. The first day of orientation, all the new students gathered in an auditorium. "Carolina in My Mind" was playing on a cheap sound system. The master of ceremonies was one of those motivational speakers. He would call out names of North Carolina towns and ask people who were from there to applaud. When he said "Charlotte," Andy moved his hands close to one another but did not let them touch. Then the guy said, "How many out-of-staters are here today?" A few people applauded, and he said, "You're all Carolinians now."

Andy wasn't sure what courses to take. His high school grades had been average, so he figured he wasn't real bright. But he knew a lot of politicians, so it made sense to major in political science.

His first class was called "Urban Politics." Students studied the structure of city and county governments. Andy memorized things like the role of a mayor in a council-manager type of government. Once in a while they would talk about campaigns, but not too often.

Andy did not have enough money to buy many political buttons anymore. All his money went for pizzas. He ordered a lot of them from the pizza delivery service because college cafeteria food was just like what he was served at home and the hospital. Andy and Ryan would go to the cafeteria together, get in line, and point at the main course.

"What is *that*?"

"That ain't nothin' but chicken-fried steak," said the cafeteria lady.

The salad bar was off limits because this big blond guy named Adolph would always put gross stuff like chicken skin in the condiments. The only good thing in the cafeteria was the soda fountain. You were allowed to make kamikazes, which were five different kinds of sodas in the same glass. Andy would drink maybe six kamikazes, choke down a bite or less of chicken-fried steak, and then go back to the dorm and order a pizza.

He once heard a story about a pizza delivery boy who was bringing a big order to the football players' dorm. A bunch of the hunks tied him up, busted his belt, and ate all his pizzas without paying him or giving him a tip. Andy wondered where this pizza boy was; he wanted to know what it had felt like.

Andy felt embarrassed when the delivery boys came to his door, especially the good-looking ones. The policy of the Delivery Depot was "delivery in less than a half-hour, or two dollars off." Even when they were an hour late, Andy didn't have the nerve to ask for a discount. And when they came on Friday and Saturday nights, Andy would pile his textbooks on local government all over his desk and pretend to be studying. He wanted to look brainy, not hard-up.

Ryan started to get to know some of the other guys in the dorm, most of whom ignored Andy. He hadn't gotten off to a good start when they saw him putting on a facial mask every night, even though it was prescription.

He was soon labeled a wimp for asking the hall counselor about getting a lock for the bathroom door and curtains for the shower stalls and toilets. Instead of being grateful, the guys called him a pussy. He did not see what was so wimpy about wanting a little privacy in the bathroom. But the guys said, "What's the matter, you don't want us to see your wong?" Andy found out that not only did guys not mind exposing themselves to each other, but a lot of them flaunted it. "I gave birth to a four-pound, two-ounce corn baby" was written in one toilet stall, with the guy's name and the date and time of day.

A few months into the first semester, the elections were held. Both Lucius Cheshire and Jimmy Carter lost. Everybody in the magazines wrote about what an asshole Jimmy Carter was and how they'd never liked him from the start. "Jimmy Carter will have a lot of time for fishing now," said one of the neutral magazines. And Hainus Rainwater said his victory proved that North Carolina was a "conservative, God-fearing state."

Andy thought about transferring to an out-of-state school as a political statement, but the sight of Ryan every morning made him stay put.

They slept in metal-frame bunk beds; Andy on top, Ryan on the bottom. Ryan would get up first (he had an 8 A.M. class), undress, go to the shower, come back. The room would be filled with the smell of soap and beer shampoo. His back would be turned to Andy. He wore nothing but boxer shorts. Andy watched as Ryan brushed his hair, watched every muscle flex with each stroke. He'd stare, take him in, make sure the bed didn't squeak. Andy moaned only when the hair dryer was on.

One night Andy and Ryan went to a PJ party. You didn't need an invitation, everybody was welcome. A PJ had nothing to do with sleeping attire. It was fruit juice mixed with grain alcohol. It tasted just like the grape juice young people had with graham crackers in elementary school.

The party was at a fraternity house. Right away, a bunch of girls came up to Ryan, took him away from Andy. Andy leaned against a wooden beam pretending to read the "Upcoming Activities" notice on the frat's cork bulletin board. After a half-hour he realized he looked like a loser or an amazingly slow reader. So he got in the line for more PJs and kept letting people get in front of him. That way, he'd still be standing with a purpose. Even when he didn't want any more to drink, he clenched the plastic Dixie cup tightly in his hands. He wouldn't know what to do with them otherwise.

He noticed lots of preppie boys wearing two shirts: a tennis shirt underneath a long-sleeved cotton button-down. They weren't hiding acne, this was the new style. Andy was going to try that, maybe get rid of some of his turtlenecks.

He was looking for a new beam to lean against when he saw Ryan across the room. Some girl was sitting on his lap, unbuttoning his shirt. He looked sexy and embarrassed. His eyes met Andy's and he mouthed something to the girl, who said, "Aw, come on, bay-bee." Ryan picked her up, put her back on the couch, walked toward Andy.

"Let's go, man," Ryan said.

"Come back, bay-bee," the girl yelled.

"I don't want to interrupt," Andy said.

"Nah, man, she's the fraternity slut, anybody could have her."

She hadn't looked at Andy, that's for sure.

When they got back to the dorm, Ryan collapsed on the lower bunk. Andy climbed into the top bunk; the bed was unmade, the sheet was in a ball, the mattress was covered with the morning's cum stains. It didn't matter, nobody else would be coming up there. Well, maybe the maintenance man would see it when he put in new overhead lighting.

"What's it like to get attention like that?" Andy asked.

"It's no big deal," Ryan said. "If you didn't stand against a pole all night, they'd be doing the same to you."

That made sense for about a minute.

Andy ran his hand over his face. He popped some zits. They made a quiet bang, like a gun with a silencer on the cop shows. Pus and blood got on his hands. His face would look worse in the morning—the open sores—but it felt good now. Getting out a lot of blood and pus. Andy thought about looking in the mirror the next morning and said to himself, I don't want to wake up. He thought maybe some kind of miracle would happen and they'd all be gone, exorcised. Then he realized the miracle had already come, he was here with Ryan. Hope. Maybe acne would become attractive, just as plumpness had been for women in Victorian times.

Andy jumped down from his bunk. He looked at Ryan, asleep with the light still on. As often as Andy stared at him, Ryan had always been awake and Andy had had to be discreet. Or Ryan had been asleep with the lights off and all Andy could do was smell him.

But now with the light on . . .

He was perfect. If it weren't for the stubble, his face could have been a woman's. His mouth was open, like a little boy's. Andy tried to find something wrong with Ryan's looks; there had to be something. His back he knew well from the mornings, but he had never gotten to stare at his chest for a long time. The girl who'd called him "bay-bee" at the party had already undone the first three buttons on his shirt. Andy undid the fourth. Ryan didn't move. The fifth, Ryan muttered something in his sleep. The last one. Andy spread the shirt apart. The chest was olive, the skin smooth and tight, the small tuft of hair that disappeared into his Levi's—Andy had seen it the first day they met—was fuller. He touched the hair, then the navel. Oh fuck, he still had pimple blood on his fingers. Andy got hard and scared at the same time. He turned out the light, jacked off, fell asleep.

Andy woke up the next morning alone. Ryan was gone. Where was he? Ryan was awake the entire time. He went to report me to the administration. No, it was Saturday. He went to tell the guy down the hall who had the corn baby, and they've locked me in the room, put pennies in the door frame. The door suddenly opened. Where had he been? The blood, Andy had gotten blood on him. What would he say? Um, you were breathing funny, you drank too much, I took your pulse. My pulse on my navel? You know how bad I am with bodies, I didn't even know where babies came from until I met you.

Ryan had a bottle of aspirin and a can of tomato juice. "Fuck, man, this is the worst hangover I've ever had. Want some?" He offered Andy some tomato juice.

"Andy, I think we've got bedbugs or something. I got a bite on my stomach last night."

"I'll get some bug spray." Andy pretended to be Gus the exterminator. They laughed.

THE personal ads in the student newspaper, *The Daily Tar Heel*, were usually for students announcing crushes (Ryan had received a couple) or looking for dates, room-mates, tickets for concerts and sporting events, rides. The ad to Andy was not intimate but just as well could have been. "Attention: Students with moderate–severe acne. Participants needed in study of new medication. . . ." It told the stricken students where to go and said money would be paid at the end of the study.

About twenty-five students sat in the waiting room of the dermatology department lab. Andy looked around. He never realized there were so many people with bad skin on campus; he'd hardly seen any of these people before, except the guy with the ski mask. He'd seen him on campus with his red-and-white ski mask covering ev-erything except his eyes. Andy thought it was some kind of fraternity dare: "Man, if you wear that ski mask for an entire semester, we'll give you three kegs." After all, the guy did have a really great body. It turned out he had really bad skin, too.

Andy looked at the sides of the other people's faces. As

many times as he'd looked at himself in the mirror, it was always head-on, never from the side. Was his skin that bad? Indented and all?

The dermatologist in charge of the study was a short, brusque Yankee woman with porcelain skin, high heels, and a white doctor's smock. She said there were two new pimple "erntments" on the verge of being approved by the federal government. "They may make your skin worse, but chances are they'll make it better. However, it's possible they'll take a lot of your skin off in the process." The ointments were free to the participants, who would be given $150 if they made it through the nine-week program. They could not sue the university if they didn't like the way things turned out. "But let's face it, you guys," the doctor said, "from the looks of things, you've got nothing to lose."

One girl started to cry. She said she thought her skin was only moderate to bad, and would just as soon go on the Pill to clear it up. Although she was against it morally, being a transfer student from a Christian college, it sure would be better than "this ugliness."

As soon as he got to his dorm room, Andy covered his face with a brown ointment. For the first time in years he could look at his face without seeing pimples. He saw just the bone structure. It wasn't bad. High cheekbones. Deep black eyes, roman nose. He liked having this even-toned mask on, even though it smelled like poop. When he reluctantly washed it off, his face was beet-red from the chemicals that hadn't been approved by the government yet. Then he applied the next ointment, a liquid that smelled like kitchen disinfectant. But his skin was so used to benzoyl peroxide, Stridex pads, and Buf·Pufs that it was like splashing on plain water.

The first time Ryan smelled the stuff he said, "Did the exterminator come?"

Andy thought of putting the ointments on his chest and back, but that would be too much to deal with. Sometimes he even took showers wearing a T-shirt. When Ryan went to bed, he just took off his shirt and pants and collapsed; he didn't even need to wash his face. To Andy, that was freedom.

By the end of the study, Andy's face was coming off. It would come off with the slightest touch. Once a piece of skin fell on a slice of pizza, but nobody noticed; the colors were similar. But at a health-food restaurant, a sliver flaked off into a cup of pure white yogurt, to the waiter's horror. It was a good thing Andy usually ate alone.

Underneath the peeling skin was not a layer of skin like Ryan's but a red face with deep marks in it. Plus Andy was still getting pimples. He took the $150. He didn't want to buy buttons with it, there had to be something better. Maybe he could go out somewhere nice on a date and have dinner. Later on.

7

ONE spring night freshman year, Ryan went to see
a punk-rock band called the Ex-Teens and afterward told
Andy the experience had changed his life. "Cool as shit."
He saw them at a new-wave club that had a pig on the roof
because it was a barbecue restaurant during the day and
early evening. Ryan told Andy he should come along the
next time a cool band came.

Ryan and Andy went to see the Go-Go's before they became famous. Each member of the band pulled up in a pink
Volkswagen. Ryan was wearing leather pants and a sleeveless T-shirt that exposed his underarm hair to the general
public. He said he was inspired by an Adam Ant video.

"That guy's fucking fantastic, I want to look like him,"
Ryan said.

"Would you kiss him?" Andy asked.

"If I was fucked up, maybe."

The Go-Go's played "We Got the Beat" and Ryan
danced. Andy had never seen him dance before. It felt
good looking at Ryan for this long and in public without
his knowing.

Andy liked some of the songs but didn't even think about dancing. He just leaned against a wall and kept peeling the label off his beer bottle until his nails were filled with moist, sticky paper. He was wearing a tennis shirt under a cotton button-down. He overheard one of the girls hanging around Ryan say, "Who's your preppie friend?" She said the word "preppie" with disgust, but it was pleasant to be called something that didn't refer to his face.

One girl who was hanging out with Ryan wore a key for an earring and had spiky hair that was mostly blond, with some black roots showing. She had on a black mini-dress and torn black hose. She and her girlfriend, who tried to look like her but was too self-conscious about it, were smoking cigarettes and staring at Ryan as he danced alone. Andy heard them saying "soooo cute" and "gorgeous." He got hard when he heard them, and he wanted to talk to them because now they had something in common. But when he stood next to the self-conscious one, both girls took a couple of steps back.

Eventually the girl with a key for an earring started dancing with Ryan. Then they started kissing. Andy thought this meant he'd have to sleep somewhere else that night. He wished he could stay at a hotel—the Tar Heel Manor or the Carolina Inn—and order room service, but he didn't have enough money.

He went into the bathroom for a long time so people wouldn't think he had been in the same spot the entire night. He didn't need to go to the bathroom, so he just sat. There were scribblings from songs like "Anarchy in the U.K." With this new-wave/punk scene, a lot of the cool people who majored in stuff like art history were talking with British accents and saying they were for anarchy, even if they voted for Ronald Reagan.

The Go-Go's stopped playing. Ryan introduced Andy

to the girl he was kissing. She was Candelabra, her friend, Silhouette. They gave Andy brief smiles that didn't show teeth and then looked away.

"Andy, can you sleep someplace else tonight?"

He knew it. "Sure, no problem."

Ryan didn't say thanks. He took Candelabra out by the arm and Silhouette followed.

Andy remembered when he had spent the night at Arthur Treacher's Fish and Chips; it wasn't all that bad. This time he'd be doing it for somebody he loved. He went to the twenty-four-hour restaurant where graduate students always came to drink a lot of coffee and stay up all night. Andy couldn't even pretend he was studying; he didn't have any books. He could pretend he was working on stuff that was already in his head, but that might make him look retarded. So he just sat there and ate a plate of jumbo onion rings as slowly as he could. His "State and Local Politics" class wouldn't be for another six hours, so that meant he had to eat one onion ring per hour.

When he was on his third, he noticed a guy at another table looking at him. The guy was built and had a pretty face, too. He was too good-looking to be in a place like this. Maybe he wasn't looking at me, Andy thought, maybe he wants ketchup for his french fries. But there wasn't any ketchup on Andy's table. Salt?

"Are you lonely?" the handsome boy asked.

Andy wasn't sure what to think, but he was already embarrassed, as though he were doing something wrong. "Beg your pardon?"

"Are you lonely?" He said it louder. Even some graduate students looked up.

"Maybe a little, I don't know."

"Have you ever thought about soul travel?"

Ryan had once asked Andy if the mind was separate

from the body, but he couldn't answer the question. Hadn't thought about it.

"No, I haven't," Andy said.

"Well, take a look at our literature." He pulled some of it from the inside of his notebook. "We're having a meeting tomorrow night. The info's on there. Maybe you'd like to come."

"Well . . ."

"Just take a look."

Andy looked at the literature, xeroxed on colored paper. At least he'd have something to do with his eyes. He was sick of looking at onion rings, and he'd already read the menu twelve times.

The literature talked about how we already possess everything we need and how much we could learn about ourselves by taking a longer look at our dreams. Also how our souls could travel.

Andy figured he had nothing to lose by going. The guy with the literature certainly didn't look like a loser. Maybe Andy would meet somebody there; it probably wouldn't be like the ladies from *The Watchtower*. Andy would need to make some new friends; he had a feeling that Candelabra was going to become Ryan's first *real* girlfriend, and she probably wouldn't want Andy hanging around.

The soul-travel meeting was in a mall near the university. Andy had never realized that a mall had meeting rooms in addition to stores and restaurants. The group using the room before the soul travelers was late breaking up. They were security people discussing shoplifting. They were arguing over whether or not they could keep the merchandise that had been "stolen" in their shoplifting skits.

There were several empty metal folding chairs around a table. Andy looked around quickly to see if the guy from the all-night restaurant was there. He was, but Andy made it a point not to sit next to him. He didn't want to appear too enthusiastic. He sat three down. The boy looked at Andy and opened his mouth. Maybe he was inviting him over?

"I'm sorry, that seat is taken," he said.

"There . . . there's nobody near it," Andy replied.

Then a big girl two chairs down motioned for Andy to sit next to her. She had black hair, permed, a pale complexion, and a black sweater and black pants. She wore a lot of makeup that made her face seem whiter. Her nails were so long and red that Andy wondered if they were store-bought. She was smoking a cigarette. From the looks of her, Andy thought she'd sound like a tough, gravelly voiced woman, but when she spoke it turned out her voice was high-pitched and southern.

"Don't be hurt," she said, looking into his eyes. "That seat you were in is reserved for the Eck Master."

She pointed to a framed photograph that had just been placed on the wall. The man in the photograph was wearing a sports jacket with lapels that reached to his shoulders. His hair was thinning and his forehead very large. He looked more like a salesman than a religious or cultural leader.

"You mean that guy in the picture is coming to this meeting?" Andy asked.

"Oh, no," she said. "They're just saving a seat to be deferential to him, sort of like saying grace before dinner."

Andy was glad she said "they." Maybe she didn't belong there, either.

He was aching to leave, but there was no way to avoid being noticed in such a small crowd.

A guy who looked like a substitute teacher got up and nodded to the man in the photograph. "Harold Garvin, the living Eck Master."

"I want to welcome you folks to our meeting. How many first-timers do we have here?"

A mousy-looking girl raised her hand. Andy remembered her from the restaurant that night. He felt used—that handsome boy was inviting *everybody* to these things. What did he do, make the rounds at coffee shops looking for people sitting by themselves? Andy didn't want to call attention to himself, so he slouched in his chair.

"I'm sure that some of you were skeptical at first about a new quote religion unquote, but what we're doing here—forgive me, James Brown—is to put the *soul* back into it. Seems religion these days has gotten to mean nothing more than bake sales and telethons. We'd like to get back to the basics, back to the soul, and we start by—it's simple enough—thinking about our dreams."

He said a number of eye-opening tapes and books teaching you how to soul travel and become a more fulfilled person were available at a low cost. "Life's storehouse of inner treasures is within your grasp. Go ahead—think of what you really want."

Andy thought of Ryan.

"It's to be a happy person, am I right? Well, you've already got it in ya, we just wanna help ya get in touch with it. We're not selling anything, because you've already got it—and no, there aren't any returns, haha."

The books stacked up on the "For Sale" table were *How to Find God, Dream Your Way to Wisdom,* and *Are You Going My Way?*

Andy was glad when the meeting was over.

The girl sitting next to him stood up just when he did. She was as tall as he was. He'd never seen a girl so tall. She said her name was Mary Alice.

Andy thought a girl this tall would like a tall guy, even if he had a bad complexion. He'd once seen a girl more than six feet tall on a television program, *The Love of My Life,* talking about how hard it was to find a "love of her life" who was as tall as she was. In other words, she never got asked out on dates. Then she heard about an organization called the Tip Top Club that everybody had to be more than six feet to join. She said she met her husband at a covered-dish supper organized by the group and they were very happy, although they did not plan to have children.

Andy said "Thanks" to the soul-travel people so Mary Alice would think he was a gentleman, and then said to her, "I think your outfit is really cool."

·"Thank you." She smiled.

They walked into the shopping part of the mall. Andy didn't want to separate, so he asked, "What did you think?" in a neutral way, to be sure not to offend.

"Well, this is my second time," she said. "I think a lot of it is silly, but at least they're discussing things that most people won't even acknowledge."

Mary Alice said that she was in psychology graduate school and that almost everybody there was real dull and too academic. "They're so grounded in their dogma that they don't see what's really going on around them. There's a whole other world out there."

Andy said, "Yeah, you're right," but he felt shallow.

As they passed the Cheese Hut, a matronly bleached-blond woman in an embroidered apron held out a tray of free cubes of cheese on toothpicks, saying, "Try our Swiss, it's delish."

They took some. "Wait here," Andy said.

He ran in and bought Mary Alice some maple candy.

"Oh, that's sweet," she said. "You shouldn't have done that."

"Just pretend it's a free sample."

They were outside and Andy started walking toward the bus stop. "I can give you a ride if you need one," Mary Alice said.

"Are you sure it wouldn't be a problem?" he asked. He told her which dorm he lived in.

It was a tight squeeze in Mary Alice's little Honda, a stick shift.

"I don't know how to use one of those," Andy said. "Oh, it's easy."

Mary Alice said one of the best things about being in graduate school was having her own place. Andy nodded, said it must be great. But ever since he'd been sharing a room with Ryan, he couldn't imagine living without him. Andy was already thinking about graduation—where would they live then? What if Ryan wanted to move in permanently with Candelabra?

They drove past some student houses. There was a little green one that had a woodcarved Christian fish sticking up in the front lawn. Instead of scales it had the words "His House" carved into it.

"I've always wanted to ask them if He was home." Mary Alice laughed.

"I'll do it," Andy said.

"You will?"

She pulled over. Andy walked up to the house, Mary Alice behind him. He knocked on the screen door. He had never done anything so bold. Somehow he'd never even rung a neighbor's doorbell and run away when he was a kid.

A slender, slightly stooped boy appeared. He wasn't intimidating, thank God.

"Pardon me, we were just wondering, Is *He* home?" Andy asked through the screen.

"Of course," the boy said matter-of-factly, with a smile. "He's always home." He opened the door. "Would y'all like to come in?"

"Oh, no, no, we were just driving by and got curious," Andy said.

The boy was so kind and earnest Andy wanted to get back in the car.

"We're having a potluck supper Thursday night. Y'all are welcome to come," the boy said.

"Thanks," said Andy.

"Thank you," said Mary Alice.

"Maybe we should have asked for some free literature," Andy said.

"We've got enough for one night."

Andy wanted to invite Mary Alice to his dorm room. He'd never brought a girl there before. He wanted Ryan to see him with her, wanted him to know that he could pick up a girl too.

He opened his mouth a few times but couldn't get himself to ask.

"It was great meeting you, Andy," Mary Alice said when they were in front of the dorm. The engine was running and she wasn't looking for a parking space.

"Would you like to come in?" he asked.

"I've got a paper to write."

Andy's face burned, not from his acne medication.

"Maybe another time, though, okay?" Mary Alice said.

That night, Andy thought how flowers had always worked with his mother. The next day he bought a bouquet from the "flower ladies," the black women who sat in folding chairs on the street with their legs spread so wide apart that you could see the clasps of their garter belts holding up their thick stockings. They sat there every day until sunset, selling flowers in old tin cans.

Andy wrote a note to go with the flowers, inviting Mary Alice to a "potluck at My house or the restaurant of your choice." He left the flowers and the invitation at the psychology grad school office.

Mary Alice said yes, and that she'd prefer a restaurant. Andy had figured she probably would. They agreed to meet at a place where the trendy professors ate. It would cost Andy the price of a couple of rare Carter buttons.

Mary Alice wasn't there. Maybe she thinks I'm supposed to meet her outside, Andy thought. But he'd already ordered a Coke and eaten some of the free bread and butter. He didn't want the waiter to think he was skipping out on the bill.

Mary Alice finally came, twenty minutes late. He stood up when the maître d' brought her to the table. In heels she was taller than Andy.

She was wearing a vintage black jacket that Andy thought would look cool on him. If we start dating, we can share clothes, Andy thought. Same size, probably.

All Andy usually thought about was politicians, Ryan, and trying to clear up his face. So hearing someone talk about poltergeists and meditation was at least different.

Ryan said there were two kinds of people: cool and uncool. Andy was sure that in Mary Alice he'd found a cool one. Ryan would probably be impressed.

Andy tossed back some wine and wondered what it would be like to kiss Mary Alice. Despite her good concealing job with rich red lipstick, he noticed her upper lip was a lot smaller than her lower one. But then Andy remembered that saying about looking a gift horse in the mouth.

He didn't want to seem pushy, and he didn't want to be rejected again, so after dinner he walked her to her car and, before she could say anything, quickly kissed the back of her hand, just the way Carolina had taught him.

"Thank you for a lovely night," he said.

Mary Alice seemed confused that he hadn't tried to kiss her on a more sensual body part. "Thank *you*," she said. "You're very sweet."

Andy wasn't too surprised when a few days later Mary Alice invited him to her apartment for dinner. (He figured since he hadn't forced himself on her, he had probably made himself more appealing in some way.) It wouldn't be the same as having her over to the dorm, which is what he really wanted, but as Andy's mother said, "It's always nice to be asked, whether you want to go or not."

Mary Alice lived in the lower-level apartment of what was once a single-family house. She had a little porch with a swing that hung from a rafter. She sat on it and invited Andy to sit down next to her. He wanted to say, "I don't think it's big enough for the two of us," but since she wasn't a guy it would probably have hurt her feelings.

As they swung, Andy looked straight ahead at the driveway and told Mary Alice about how he tended to get motion sickness on rides and swings, how he got carsick every vacation, how he got whacked on the head with pre-algebra textbooks on bus rides all of junior high.

"Good Lord, that sounds awful," she said. "But at least you talk about your pain. Most guys don't do that."

Andy wanted to get off the swing. "Well, something sure smells good."

"Let's eat," Mary Alice said.

She had fixed a dinner of melted Muenster cheese on melba toast and opened a bottle of white wine. She had her melba toast plain. This was the kind of food Andy's mother ate, but had she served it on dates back when she was courting? No wonder she hadn't gotten many guys.

They had sugarless gum for dessert, and Mary Alice said, "Let's sit on the couch." They did.

Mary Alice asked Andy if he wanted more wine. He knew what that meant, so he excused himself.

"May I use the sandbox?" he asked. That was so much nicer than saying "I have to take a leak" or "Time to take a dump," like the guys at the dorm, and it was good for a laugh.

Andy locked the bathroom door and turned on the

faucet. He pulled his pants down most of the way and lay facedown on the cold bathroom tile. The bathroom was only about six feet long so he had to put his feet up over the edge of the bathtub. He thought about how much nicer it was to jack off in bed. He visualized Ryan half-naked, standing still. But he couldn't concentrate. He had to answer to someone else. He pulled his pants up, flushed the toilet, turned off the faucet. He came out into the now dark room, squinting and sniffing. Mary Alice had lit some candles and was burning incense. He tripped over her feet, knocking down one of the candles. Quickly he blew out the candle, and instead of saying, "Oh, I hope I didn't burn the carpet," he started kissing her.

He began on the nape of her neck, slowly moving up to her cheeks, her eyes, her eyebrows. She put her mouth on his. He put his tongue in her mouth, but all he felt were teeth, probably because of her funny lip. He stopped, trying not to be abrupt or obvious, and asked if he could kiss her pineapple, and she laughed. She didn't make him laugh or get hard. He kept trying.

He undid her shirt, she unhooked her bra. Her boobs were big and warm and comfortable. It felt good to rest on them. She didn't want to rest.

"Why do you wear so many shirts?" she asked.

Andy said it was the layered look, part of the new conservatism.

She started unbuttoning his shirt, so he quickly put his mouth on one of her boobs, sucked on it gently until all of it was in his mouth. Its size varied, depending on how much of it he sucked in. She put her hands on his pants, but there was nothing there but a wallet. He put his head back on her boobs, slid his body down enough to protect himself.

"Let's not rush things," Andy said. "It's so good just to be with you."

CANDELABRA'S roommate flunked out and moved back home, so Ryan started staying over at Candelabra's place. Andy didn't need to see Ryan to get off; just thinking about him was enough. And he didn't have to worry about the bed squeaking.

Now Andy was able to go through Ryan's drawers, see if he had any secret scribblings. He found a photo-booth picture of Ryan passionately kissing Candelabra. His tongue was in her mouth, he could tell. It was the best picture Andy had ever seen, better than the one of Preston and him with Jimmy Carter. The whole side of a Blondie album played while he stared at it. That would be the best feeling in the world, he thought: to have Ryan's tongue in my mouth.

Andy went through Ryan's side of the chest of drawers and found a pair of Candelabra's panties—they must have been hers—in a department store box with some cards that she'd sent him. Ryan must really like this girl, Andy thought. He sure didn't want to keep a pair of Mary Alice's undies around.

Since they hardly ever saw one another anymore, Ryan and Andy communicated through notes they'd leave on each other's desks. Who'd called, what records they were going to buy, who owed how much on the phone bill. One day Andy wrote Ryan a note saying "I miss you, let's have dinner or something." Instead of "A" or "Andy," he signed it: "I love you, Andy."

Ryan came in late that night. He slept over maybe once a week now. Andy was almost asleep, the lights were out. He heard Ryan pull the chain on the little fluorescent light on his desk. He's seeing it now, Andy thought. Then he heard a piece of paper being ripped, again and again. Andy never knew a piece of paper could be ripped into so many little pieces.

It's no big deal, Andy thought to himself. It's not like I tried to kiss him or something.

Ryan never said anything about the note. Whenever Andy saw him, he was in a pretty good mood, so it couldn't have bothered him that much. Maybe because he was getting more and more into pot. He'd buy a whole bag and pick out the sticks and seeds. Sometimes you could still hear the seeds popping when he used a pipe.

Ryan took a lot of chemistry classes, so he was able to get some plastic tubing and a beaker and make his own bong. He loved showing it off, and there was nothing that Andy liked better than sharing the bong with Ryan, who was getting even prettier since he'd been dating Candelabra. She was an art major, so she got him to wear real hip new-wave clothing and an earring.

They'd pass the bong back and forth and say stuff like "Suck on this" and giggle. Andy wondered if Ryan knew how good he looked.

With Ryan so stoned, Andy didn't need to get very high. He sucked in only a little bit and pushed the smoke out of his mouth quickly. But Ryan did it properly; he got a cotton mouth. "I'll wet it for ya," Andy would say. They laughed.

One night Andy and Ryan were walking across campus. When they passed the jock dorm a guy yelled, "Hey, faggot!" Andy turned around. But then he realized it was aimed at Ryan, the pretty boy with the earring.

Mary Alice was impressed that Andy's roommate was a punk rocker and said she wanted to meet the girl with the wild name, Candelabra. "She must have a lot of creative energy," she said.

Thinking about Ryan and all the attention he was getting from Candelabra made Andy depressed. "I feel so ugly," he said to Mary Alice. "My skin is so fucked up."

"Come on," she said. "It's not that bad."

She took Andy by the hand into her bathroom. She rummaged through bottles of nail polish, cans of hair spray, lipsticks, eyeliner pencils, and eye shadow in the cabinet and finally found an old bottle of foundation.

"Mine's too light for you, but we'll try this. I use it when I've got a tan."

She dotted it on Andy's forehead, nose, and cheeks. Then she blended it all together with her hands. Nobody had ever touched him like that, for any reason. "Fabulous," she said.

Andy looked in the mirror. A few lumps and indentations were still visible but the skin tone was even, "porcelain beige," not pimple red.

"God, thanks, Mary Alice," he said. Andy was so grateful that he kissed her right there in the bathroom. Then he took off her shirt, started sucking on the boobs. At last he got it up. He wanted to fuck her standing up; they were the same height, after all. He took off his pants, but it was too complicated. They went to her bed.

He kissed her all over, everywhere except on the lips. He couldn't stop saying "I love you so much," because he felt as if he did. He got inside her, even found it with the lights out. It was moist and he lasted a long time. She moaned, but after a while he got bored and started to count his thrusts. He was supposed to come but couldn't.

When she finished moaning he knew he was allowed to stop. He was still hard and wished he could go home and masturbate, release.

He fell asleep on her boobs.

"Good morning, lover," Mary Alice said.

It was light, so Andy ran to get his shirt.

There was blood on the sheets; at last it wasn't from pimples.

He made sure Mary Alice did his makeup before they went out for breakfast together at Ye Olde Waffle Shoppe. They sat at the counter and held hands while the grill master scrambled their eggs.

8

MARY ALICE gave Andy a book about a man who had been an uptight professor and a repressed homosexual until he took a hunk of acid. Then he moved to India, became a holy man, and was very calm. He made a lot of money lecturing in college towns on trips back to the United States. Mary Alice was so fascinated by this man's spiritual journey that she started talking about going to India over the summer. Andy was intrigued too, but he didn't want to travel any farther than the room he shared with Ryan.

The first time Andy heard about acid was in psychology class in high school. The teacher, Mr. Perkins, didn't like to talk, so he showed a lot of instructional films, not necessarily about psychology. The best one was about the evils of acid.

It was narrated by Sonny Bono and warned about the dangers of taking acid, which included losing your mind, making a fool of yourself in front of your peers at a party, and killing yourself without knowing it at the time. The film tried to show what the effects were like by making everything go crazy after one of the actors dropped some acid. At first everybody in the class thought the film was spliced and that they'd have to watch *Bear Country*, a nature movie, instead. But the class realized it was special effects when a deep, distorted voice chanted, "Acid, acid," like it was coming from a well filled with polluted water.

The film reminded Andy of Art Linkletter's daughter, who jumped out of a window and passed away after taking acid.

Ryan had once told Andy that he'd try anything once. "Well, *almost* anything," he'd said. So maybe Ryan would be impressed if Andy got them some acid. Andy asked Mary Alice how he could get some. She said she didn't want to take any herself—although Andy never asked—but she suggested she could "monitor" him while he tripped. He said maybe.

"I could probably get you some from Jacob," she said. "But please be careful. My girlfriend Donna walked in front of a car the last time she did it."

"Did she die?"

"No, but she's got to wear a neck brace."

Mary Alice came through. Two tiny bits of navy-blue blotter, smaller than a one-cent postage stamp, with a little orange triangle in the middle.

"Please call me while y'all are doing this," she said.

"Sure, sure," said Andy.

"Maybe *I* should do it with you, instead of Ryan."

"Nah, I hardly ever get to see him anymore. Besides, *you* don't need these kinds of things for your soul."

She nodded and sighed.

Andy and Ryan decided to drop that very night. Andy went to the gourmet cookie shop for some of Ryan's favorites—large chocolate chip cookies folded and filled with fudge icing. Then he stopped at the record shop and bought a twelve-inch import by a synthesizer band that

Ryan had been wanting. When he got home, he took a shower, put on a sleeveless T-shirt, a pair of shorts, and some of the makeup Mary Alice had bought for him. Looking in the small, toothpaste-specked mirror in his room, he remembered Mary Alice's advice: "Blend carefully and beware the lines."

When Ryan finally came in he was all excited. He said Candelabra couldn't believe he'd never tried the stuff before.

"She's kind of pissed that I'm not doing it with her, but she's going to the Swimming Pool Q's concert in Raleigh, so she's over it." The Swimming Pool Q's sang a song about Cream of Wheat cereal that had a dance beat.

They sat on Ryan's bed and put the little squares of paper on their tongues. "Suck on it a long time, that's what we're supposed to do," Andy said. He started to feel as if he'd taken a whole bottle of NoDoz.

"Don't worry." Andy knew he was being too protective. "It's not like Diane Linkletter. We don't even have a window." The inside of the dorm was made entirely of yellow-painted cinder blocks. Even if they jumped from the top bunk, there was a carpet remnant to cushion them.

Andy realized what he had taken was more than a bunch of NoDoz when he suddenly saw spider webs between his fingers.

Ryan put on the new record Andy had brought home.

It sounded so good they decided that's where they wanted to live, where the music came from.

"But where is that?" Ryan asked.

Before Andy could answer, he found himself tumbling onto the carpet, brushing against Ryan but feeling no desire. It was like when he was little, before the pimples, when he was allowed to touch his idols, his little plaster presidents.

Then they started talking: This is what death is

like / Death is freedom / Since Hitler killed the Jews he was actually freeing them and must have loved them / The same goes for Idi Amin / Their new mission was to spread love / How would they spread the word / Ryan will be the thinker, on account of his high grades / Andy the leader on account of his political contacts.

It was getting late. They should call their girlfriends. Andy went first. Ryan held his head close to the receiver so he could listen in. Andy wasn't feeling like a little boy anymore; the whole room smelled of Ryan. Their hair touched. Mary Alice answered on the first ring.

"I'm *so* glad you called," she said. "I was getting worried. How's the trip?"

"We're flying," Andy said.

"I sure wish you could fly over here. Mind if I come over?"

Andy and Ryan looked at each other, shook their heads at the same time.

Andy's yawn came easily. "Nah, I think we're gonna crash soon. I'll see you tomorrow."

Ryan tried to get Candelabra, but she wasn't back from the Swimming Pool Q's concert.

Andy wanted to test him.

"Maybe she met a guy there."

"Nah," Ryan said.

"Maybe one of those guys in the band."

"So?"

Ryan was wearing a punk T-shirt that said "The Future Is Unwritten." Maybe there was hope.

They both lay on the floor. Ryan's smell was so sweet Andy wished he could taste it.

It seemed natural for Andy to put his head on Ryan's chest. It felt hard, not at all like Mary Alice's. Ryan looked straight up at the ceiling. Andy moved his head down to Ryan's stomach. It was softer. Even through his shirt,

Andy could feel the hairs around Ryan's navel; against his cheek he could almost count each one.

Andy was where he wanted to be. Maybe he could wish the two of them away, right now. No, he had to pee.

His pee came out all different colors, all pastel. He'd read that something like this might happen. He looked at his face in the mirror. It was one big red pustule with indentations, bloodshot eyes, and a bad brown paint job. It's the drug, Andy said to himself.

He fell asleep with his head on Ryan's chest.

"FUCK, man, what time is it?" Ryan asked.

It was over, time to wake up.

Ryan called Candelabra right away and started talking quietly in a throaty, sexy voice. "Maybe I can come over now."

Andy called Mary Alice as soon as Ryan was off the phone but didn't make plans. He'd rather be alone.

THE next time they were together in their room, Andy asked Ryan when he wanted to drop again. "How about Friday?"

"Maybe," Ryan said. "But let's all four of us do it—me, you, Candelabra, and Mary Alice." Andy felt as if he'd been turned down for a date with a bad excuse, like when girls in high school said they had to help their mothers clean the house on Friday nights. "Company's comin'," one girl had said. "We've got to beat the rug."

"I'm not sure Mary Alice would want to," Andy said. "She's still kind of bummed out about her friend being run over while she was on the stuff."

"You mean that goofy-looking chick with the neck brace?"

"That's the one."

"Well, maybe we can do it in a field or golf course, where there's no traffic," Ryan said.

"What if we get caught?"

"Man, you're too damn uptight."

"*I am not!* I just know Mary Alice won't go for it. Fuck it, you and Candelabra do it by yourselves." Andy was embarrassed at the way he sounded.

"Man, you're not jealous, are you? Wax"—that's what Ryan had started calling Candelabra—"says that it seems like you're in love with me."

Didn't he remember the "I love you" note?

"Are you?" Ryan asked.

It wasn't worth it. "No," Andy said quietly.

Ryan brought the bong to his lips, lit it, inhaled, held his head back, closed his eyes. That's when he looked his prettiest—his head tilted back, the light shining on his tiny Adam's apple, a slight smile on his face, like he was in rapture. Andy got to look at him a couple of seconds longer when Ryan took a real long hit.

"Yes," Andy said even more quietly.

Ryan didn't hear him. "Your turn." He handed Andy the bong.

"I just want to be closer to you," Andy said.

"Oh, man."

"Can we do what we did last Friday? I like being near you."

"You can if you want, but I'm not into it."

Andy started to cry.

He hadn't cried since Preston had hit him over the head on the bus with his pre-algebra book. Then he had held it all in until he was home. But now he was already home—there was nowhere else he really wanted to go.

"Man." Ryan shook his head. "I'm going over to see Wax."

After that, Andy pretty much moved in with Mary Alice. They shared makeup and clothes. Andy thought that if he was never in the dorm room, maybe Ryan would miss him, might at least want to smoke pot with him. Sometimes Andy and Mary Alice would be fucking and the phone would ring and he would jump, praying it was Ryan. It reminded him of that Vikki Carr song his mother listened to, "It Must Be Him." Mary Alice said let it ring, but Andy would always pick up.

"You don't have to answer it," she would say breathlessly.

"What if it's an emergency?" he'd say.

She thought he was real conscientious.

Andy wrote a note to himself: "Must change life or go insane."

Andy and Mary Alice did everything a couple was supposed to do. She even stopped talking about going to India by herself. But if things got too cute or if he thought Mary Alice was having too good a time, he felt embarrassed, a little sick. Like the time they were making s'mores, graham crackers with roasted marshmallows and melted chocolate. She was throwing marshmallows at him while he melted the chocolate. It was hard for him to throw them back and call this six-foot-two-inch girl "my little campfire marshmallow."

Andy started having trouble getting it up. Mary Alice didn't seem concerned. "It's from lasting so long before, probably. You just need a break," she said. She smiled and said her girlfriends said their boyfriends didn't last *nearly* as long.

When Andy did get it up, it was the kind of hard-on a guy gets in the morning, more an appendage than anything else, no tingling.

132

"Let's be friends," he said to Mary Alice.

Mary Alice wrote a note to Andy: "Our love is like the Eagles song 'I Can't Tell You Why' . . . we cannot go from lovers to friends with a simple declaration."

In other words, he'd have to move back into the dorm. If only he could find a way to make Ryan seem less attractive. Maybe then everything would be okay.

Ryan had talked about getting a mohawk. Indian warriors used to have them, but now it was punk to get your hair cut to the scalp with just a fin standing in the middle. If Ryan looked like that, Andy could stop staring at him and find something new to concentrate on.

Andy said he saw a picture of the Clash in *Creem*. Joe Strummer had a mohawk.

"What the fuck," Ryan said.

He took off his shirt and they went into the bathroom. Andy ran an electric razor against the black hair he'd longed to run his fingers through. He left a big chunk in the middle and put in gobs of Dippity-do to make it stand up, finlike. Then he put some shaving cream on the stubble that was left, pressing his chest against Ryan's shoulder just barely—he knew how to get away with it— without looking at himself in the mirror. I'll never want to touch him again, Andy thought. Now he looks awful.

More arty girls, even the lead singer of the Ex-Teens, started following Ryan around. He had the coolest cut on campus. They gave him free acid, mushrooms, and coke. Wax started getting jealous. One night she and Ryan had a fight over it, so he slept in the dorm. Andy quietly jumped down from the bunk and stared down at him as he slept.

Nothing has changed a bit, Andy thought as he wiped the cum off his hands with a T-shirt. Nothing at all.

9

ANDY returned to his candidates. The student paper let him on as a political reporter. His first article was about the decline of liberalism, and he got to interview a former congressman who was now lecturing on campus. "I played paddleball with Ted Kennedy, you know," the congressman said. Andy sent the article with his byline to his mother.

He got a lot of ideas for his stories from *Inside D.C.*, a biweekly political newsletter he subscribed to. He saw an advertisement for it in *American Politics*. The ad had a picture of the editor, Lanier Ocram, who looked like an Irish sumo wrestler. Next to his picture was a list of important subscribers that included about every politician Andy had ever dreamed of.

Andy signed up for a free two-month trial subscription to this very exclusive-sounding newsletter. It was printed like a confidential memo and addressed to "Our Clients." At the bottom, it said that the information contained in it was for the "sole private use of our clients." It had gossip about the candidates, and it even wrote about some of their personality traits. Ronald Reagan prized loyalty, for example.

The newsletter cost more than a hundred dollars a year, so when the trial period was over, Andy wrote Mr. Ocram a letter. He said he was a college student, and while he wasn't blowing all his federal government loan money on T-bone steaks (like Ronald Reagan said), he still couldn't afford the full price. Mr. Ocram wrote back saying he could have it at a student rate, twenty-five dollars.

Andy liked calling Mr. Ocram for quotes for his articles. Even when his assignments were only about campus or town politics, he found some excuse to quote him. Mr. Ocram always took his calls. He seemed eager to talk to a college boy. "Come on up and see me the next time you're in Washington," he said at the end of one telephone interview. People had told Andy that on the phone he sounded cute.

As many times as he had written and called the nation's capital, Andy had never been there in the flesh. He had once hoped to go with the high school marching band. He thought they might need someone to play the recorder, but they were short only on a baton twirler for the fife corps.

After Andy interviewed him over the phone about Jimmy Carter and the role of former presidents in present-day politics, Mr. Ocram said, "Andy, you really should come see me. I could use an intern for the summer." Andy could tell he was drinking something; he heard ice clinking in a glass. Mr. Ocram started complaining about how some big wig had talked to a gay political group and hid from by the press afterward. "What a hypocrite." Then he told some other political stories.

Andy just said "Wow" and agreed with everything he said. Mr. Ocram spoke so fast, was so excited by his own words, that he talked right over Andy's exclamations.

They agreed that Andy should come up one day over spring break.

The *Inside D.C.* offices were inside Mr. Ocram's home, a three-story town house on Capitol Hill. A beautiful black lady named Sheila let him in. Her skin was smooth as pudding. "Go on upstairs," she said.

Mr. Ocram's place was a lot like Andy's bedroom at his parents' house. There were buttons and posters everywhere, pictures of Mr. Ocram with the candidates. But here the men looked comfortable, not posed. They all knew one another, you could tell.

Mr. Ocram sat curled up, phone in hand, on a huge couch that wrapped halfway around the room. He was wearing a T-shirt with red stains and pants that were several sizes too large and bunched up at the waist with a worn leather belt. He had lost a lot of weight since his picture had been taken for that ad. His socks were mismatched—one dark blue, one black—and he wore no shoes. Clumps of hair stuck out on either side of his head like little horns. His lips were red, the same color as the stains on his shirt. Hawaiian Punch.

He looked at Andy briefly and went on with the phone conversation Andy had interrupted. Andy felt dumb standing, so he sat down on the couch—there was plenty of room. Mr. Ocram was real animated as he talked; pushing up his glasses, eating popcorn, drinking and spilling juice.

"I'll tell ya who the next president will be," he was saying. His voice was more nasal in person, and he sniffed a lot as he spoke about a Louisiana senator Andy knew all about. The senator had once sent Andy a picture postcard of his family. He had a fine-looking son.

Before he left for Washington, Andy's mother had warned him on the phone about minding his manners with successful political types: "Don't eat your peas with a knife." But it didn't look like he had much to worry about. This was not going to be a formal interview.

Mr. Ocram got off the phone, shook hands quickly with Andy. He looked a little disappointed.

Andy said quickly, "That was some race in Louisiana last year. *Nobody* thought it would be that close."

They started talking about Senate campaigns, and Andy mimicked Hainus Rainwater's wife talking about sex education. Mr. Ocram was impressed that Andy knew so much gossip about Governor and Mrs. Cheshire. Andy showed Mr. Ocram his clippings from the student paper, even his picture with Jimmy Carter and Preston.

"Who's that boy in the middle?" Mr. Ocram asked.

"A boy I knew in junior high school, Mr. Ocram."

"Call me Lanier," he said. "Listen, my secretary, Sheila, is only working part-time this summer, so I could use another hand," he said.

"Great," Andy said. The only time Andy had been worried about getting the job was when Lanier first laid eyes on him.

Mr. Ocram had an appointment, so he took Andy back to the airport, reading the *Washington Post* as he drove. He nearly ran into a man in a blue blazer and khakis scurrying across Pennsylvania Avenue as they drove past the Capitol dome.

"Doesn't it give you goose bumps?" asked Andy.

"What, running over politicians?"

"No, the Capitol."

"No," said Lanier.

Lanier went back to reading the paper, slowing down only a little. See you in May, they agreed.

Ryan picked Andy up from the Raleigh/Durham airport. He was wearing a new earring. This one was about four inches long and wobbled under his earlobe. His hair had grown back from the mohawk, and now he wore it short with extra-stiff gel—just like the boy everybody had called "Porcupine" in Andy's elementary school. The fat red laces in his high-top sneakers were undone, the new style.

Ryan smelled like pot. There was no Breathalyzer test for that, so at least they wouldn't get arrested if they got pulled over. He had borrowed Candelabra's car, a little Mustang. A beat box on the floor of the passenger seat pumped out the Dead Kennedys.

"Aren't you going to ask me how it went?"

Ryan looked at Andy and smiled.

"I got the job," Andy said.

"Wow." Ryan was really stoned. "How do you like my new earring?" He fondled it.

"You look like a real fag," Andy said.

They didn't say anything else.

In May, Andy took a room in a house owned by a lady who said she was an actress. He gave her two months' rent to start. The house was right on Capitol Hill, so Andy could walk to Lanier's.

His first morning of work, Sheila was already in, typing Lanier's newsletter on the word processor. She looked flawless. Her skin was as fine as Carolina's, and her perfume smelled so good Andy wanted a bottle himself.

Sheila said Lanier wasn't up yet, but that he'd probably be yelling down to her soon. "He's probably forgotten today's your first day."

Then a skinny boy, pretty and tough looking at the same time, came downstairs pulling the bottom of his tank top up from his tight Levi's to wipe the sleep out of his eyes. Andy had never seen a guy with a waist so small.

"Eighty-five," the boy said to Sheila.

"Don't bullshit me, boy," she said. She wrote out a check for sixty dollars on the *Inside D.C.* account.

"Just make it out to 'Billy,'" the boy said. He didn't look at Andy, didn't even seem to notice all the political pictures. He let himself out.

"Well," Sheila said. "I might as well be the one to tell you. Lanier is gay."

"Oh?" Andy said.

"This city is full of fools and sycophants who love to get the dirt on people they're inferior to. If anybody asks you anything about Lanier, I suggest you do what I do. You just tell them it's none of their damn business and ask what *they* wake up to in the morning."

"Yes ma'am," Andy said.

"Don't call me 'ma'am.'"

Andy wanted to yell. He couldn't believe his luck. He was working for a gay man in Washington, D.C. He excused himself to use the bathroom, turned on the faucet, jumped up and down. He was looking through the bathroom drawers to get a feel for the place when he saw a bottle of foundation. This was too much. Lanier was gay *and* wore makeup. But then he looked at the label, "Deep Almond," and realized it had to be Sheila's.

When Andy opened the bathroom door, Sheila went on, talking as she typed. "The man's eccentric. But he sure knows everybody in this town. You'll never have any trouble finding a job after you've worked for him."

"What do you want to do after this?" Andy asked.

"Find a man and have a baby." She was looking, too.

Then another boy came downstairs. Beautiful, perfectly put together. Andy had never seen a living person with clothes so well pressed.

Andy stared. He had to force himself to be conscious of his mouth to keep it from dropping open.

"Sean, this is Andy; Andy, Sean."

Sean looked up at Andy, tilted his head to one side, and looked him in the eyes. "Pleasure," he said breathily, extending a small hand to Andy. They shook. With the same inflection and voice he said, "Good morning, Sheila," then slid across the floor and went out the door. He was like a dancer, and Sheila and Andy were the morning's first audience.

Andy went to the window. Sean had already gotten on his red motor scooter. His little white helmet was on, his bangs still visible. His slightly rounded ass, perfectly molded by soft cotton pants, pressed softly against the leather seat. He drove away.

"That's Lanier's roommate," Sheila said. "I don't write his checks, Lanier does."

"He's very beaut . . . handsome," Andy said. He hoped Sheila wouldn't be offended that he'd noticed.

"Don't mess with him," she said.

Finally Lanier came downstairs. He was wearing a stained bathrobe without a sash. You could see his underpants; they were jockeys that were too big. They came down ridiculously far, farther than any well-endowed male's.

"Lanier, you remember Andy."

"Oh, yeah," he said. "No calls today, I'm going back to bed."

ONE of Andy's first assignments was to get things ready for a party Lanier was throwing for a friend of his, a former presidential candidate who was considered the funniest congressman in town. Andy had written to the man, and he'd written back, but only with form letters.

Still, this would be Andy's first chance to meet in a private home someone he'd written to.

Andy had to order the liquor and have it delivered, count the glassware, call the invitees or their secretaries to see who was coming, and most important, keep the guests from wandering up to the third-floor living quarters.

Andy found out that Lanier's pants were too big because he had lost so much weight on his "cocaine diet."

"He was so big I used to have to book two airline seats for him, until he started doing the toot. Now he's never hungry," Sheila said. "*And* he says it makes him more creative. To each his or her own."

Andy wore black pegged pants, a white shirt, skinny tie, white socks, and black loafers to the party. He didn't have a jacket. Almost all the guests were in their forties and wore formal suits, blue shirts, and ties with some shade of red in them. Most of the journalists there had beards and aviator glasses. Andy leaned against the kitchen wall a lot of the time, watching the stairs as he'd been told to do. A couple of times he had to say, "Um, the bathroom is down here and there's another downstairs, sir." He said that to a young guy who didn't seem to be part of the party at all. "I'm a private guest," he said with a long, forced sigh.

In his black-and-white attire, Andy was mistaken several times for a lazy waiter. People with disapproving looks kept asking him for more canapés. Andy figured, Go with it, and handed out some finger food, all the while keeping an eye on the stairwell.

Twenty or so men in nearly identical outfits gathered around the congressman, who was seated in a rocking chair. Even if they were in an uncomfortable position (like right next to the stereo speaker), they would laugh loudly at all his jokes.

They would all start laughing at the exact same time and

end at the same time, about five seconds later. The congressman rocked back and forth, told joke after joke, until one of the better-known journalists, whom everybody called by his last name—Sloan—kept laughing, beyond the five seconds. Slowly his laugh turned into a horrible cough that wouldn't stop. Even though there was no smell, it reminded Andy of his grandmother's not being able to eat a sit-down meal with his family.

Lanier pulled Andy aside. His bloodshot eyes almost bulged out as he told Andy he didn't want any 911 people coming to the house. "Get him a glass of water and drive him out of here," he whispered.

Andy was happy to do it; he'd been reading the guy's syndicated column for years.

People had started fidgeting and jingling their change once the coughing started, and now they were starting to leave, even though the water had helped Sloan pipe down.

A mucusy handkerchief, crusty with age, hung from a side pocket of Sloan's rumpled, baggy suit. He smelled strongly of cigarette smoke, which was probably why he was so sick in the throat at this point in his life. Andy did not want to suggest this to him and get into a conflict-of-interest situation. Tobacco was the number-one cash crop in North Carolina.

Sloan said he didn't want a ride, he'd just walk up Pennsylvania Avenue and get a cab. "I'm no invalid, I can take care of myself. I don't need a ride home from any goddamned caterer."

"I'm not the caterer, sir."

"Weren't you the one sticking that goddamned fairy food in my face? That's what made me so fucking sick!"

"I work for Lanier."

"You look too damned ugly for that."

Andy had thought Sloan was one of those gruff journalists with a heart of gold underneath it all, but this was too much.

As soon as Andy put the key into the ignition of Lanier's car, he realized it was a stick shift. He told Sloan he didn't know how to work one and left him in the dark garage. Just as he went to get Lanier, Sean came down the stairs and went into the garage.

"Who is that hideous old man throwing a fit in the car?" he asked Andy.

"Oh, that's Sloan. I'm supposed to drive him home, but I can't work a stick shift."

"You left him in the garage?"

"Yeah."

Sean rolled his eyes and said he'd take the old man home; he wanted the car anyway. Andy asked if he could come along. Sean said okay.

"What is the meaning of this?" Sloan said.

"Oh, get over it," Sean said.

When they dropped Sloan off in front of his fancy Georgetown apartment complex, a young doorman who looked almost as good as Sean approached the car, winked, and said "Hiiii, Sean." Sloan had to open the car door himself. He glared at Andy and started hacking again as he walked into the lobby.

Andy didn't get into the front seat. He knew he didn't look good, especially from the side. And Sean didn't ask him to sit up front. He didn't say a word.

"So how did you meet Lanier?" Andy finally asked.

"At a party," Sean said. "We were introduced."

He said he and Lanier were just friends, that he hated people thinking that they were involved romantically. Andy figured Sean had to lie because he was ashamed of having a fat, bald rich man for a boyfriend when he was beautiful and young. At least in public, anyway.

"So are you interested in politics?" Andy asked.

"God, no. It's such a hideous bore. All these men arguing about who they want for president. They decide whatever it's going to be in the end, anyway. What's the use?"

Sean said he wanted to save money, move to New York, do some modeling, and take classes at the Fashion Institute of Technology.

They stopped at a Häagen-Dazs for ice cream cones. Whenever he passed a Häagen-Dazs, Andy thought about what somebody back home said about that foreign-sounding name: "It don't mean nothin'." The slim college boy behind the counter kept his eyes on Sean the whole time he was scooping up his deep chocolate fudge. He didn't even charge him for it. Andy remembered how at the Burger Chef they had to count the cups to see how many beverages had been sold in a day. He wondered if they did the same with sugar cones.

Andy and Sean were walking down Wisconsin Avenue, past some punk boutique that had black leather belts with silver bullet studs and all kinds of cool sunglasses in the window. Andy wished Ryan could see him now; he wouldn't have to know it wasn't a date.

"So where do you want the infamous Lanier to lead you?" Sean asked.

"I don't know, somewhere in politics. I've got other stuff on my mind now."

"Like?"

"I'm sort of obsessed with my roommate back home."

"A guy?"

"Yes."

"That's funny, you don't seem the type."

"What do you mean?"

"I don't know. You just don't seem gay."

Either Sean hadn't noticed his makeup, which was a good sign, or Andy needed a smaller waist and better-pressed clothing.

"I'm going to a new dance club. You're welcome to come," Sean said.

Before they were even inside the club, Sean ran into some people he knew—boys and girls—and kissed them on both cheeks. He started talking in French, switched back to English to introduce Andy, then went back to French. Andy wasn't sure what to do with himself when those people spoke. His hands and arms felt ridiculously long, as though they weren't his. He'd noticed how uptight people either keep their arms down stiffly at their sides or hold one arm straight down with the hand of the other clutching the elbow. So he made it a point to put both hands in his back pockets, real casual. In his stomach he could feel the disco throbs from the club.

The discotheque air was thick with moist smoke from a dry-ice machine and the combined smell of men's cologne and cigarettes. Andy was afraid what the man-made smoke would to do his makeup. Then, looking around at all the pretty and muscular guys, he got even more self-conscious and found an empty wall space.

Sean was on the other side, nodding and smiling at people.

"Where do you know those French people from?" Andy asked.

"What?"

"Where do you know those French people from?"

The music was very loud, and some members of the gay community were screaming along with the song.

"What?"

"Where do you know those French people from?!"

"They're not French, they're Moroccan."

Sean started dancing. After a few minutes Andy got up the nerve to join him. He had never danced before, so he tried to visualize disco commercials he'd seen on TV. The entire disco lesson kit (available if you gave your credit card number to a toll-free operator) contained a step-by-step lesson book, a special disco dance tape, and plastic footprints you could stick on to any linoleum floor until you had memorized the latest fashionable dance. The only one Andy could recall clearly was the slap, which involved lightly slapping the face of your dance partner while "moving your feet to the disco beat." But he didn't feel familiar enough with Sean to try it with him, since he might take it the wrong way. And because he was a lot taller than Sean, he'd be slapping downward, and it just might seem he had the limp wrists he had been discouraged from having as a youth.

Andy danced for only half of a song. When Sean got off the dance floor, Andy asked him, "Um, what percentage of gay men have anal sex?" He was doing a lot of percentage figuring, analyzing Senate races for Lanier. He figured Sean might know.

"I don't know, more than half." Sean went back to dance.

Andy walked around the place; he knew he was supposed to make eye contact. No luck. He remembered his mother, when she told him she'd rather have him crippled than queer. What if he were crippled, in a wheelchair—would it be easier than this? Handicapped people probably made eye contact whenever they came across one another.

He went up to the roof of the club and looked out at the District of Columbia spread around him. He could see the Washington Monument. He thought about taking a cab there and jumping off of it, but then he remembered the tourists and how long a wait it would be just to get in, let alone climb the stairs to the top.

Back by the dance floor, Andy said to himself, Think positive, something could happen. He wanted to leave. But he wouldn't let himself. He'd say, Wait until the next

146

song, it may be good. Then count to sixty and go. He lasted through another five songs and headed for the neon exit sign as the sixth began.

Suddenly Sean bumped into him, looked up, and said, "Take me home," in a dazed, flirtatious way. It was like three hours in a gay disco had changed his entire personality.

"You've got a car, Sean."

"My gums are numb and I'm drunk," he said. "I need a cab."

"What about Lanier's car?"

"Leave it."

Sean ran into the street, looking for a cab. Andy held him back with one arm, raising the other to hail a taxi. Sean's body was flat, almost hollow. Andy could feel that he had a lot of hairs on his chest.

A cab with "Jules Massey" and a phone number painted on it pulled over. Sean and Andy got in the backseat. It was dark and Sean was fucked up. Andy wasn't so worried about how he looked.

Sean went straight for Andy's shirt and started unbuttoning it from the bottom, thank God. Andy pushed him back, and then Sean kissed him. Sean smelled like rum. They were right by the Capitol when Sean told the driver to pull over. He stuck his his head out the window and ralphed. It was a good thing the cab wasn't air-conditioned, Andy thought. The windows would have been closed.

"What the fuck are y'all doin' to my cab?"

Andy looked out the window. The throw-up was watery, and it fell on the street. It hadn't touched the cab.

"It's all right, Mr. Massey," Andy said. "It missed the car."

Andy took out five dollars and gave it to the black man. "My cousin's spleen is out of whack."

"Shit," said Mr. Massey.

Sean put his head on Andy's lap, and Mr. Massey put the car back in drive.

When they got to Lanier's house, Sean said, "Oh no, I've lost my keys." So Andy unlocked the door and helped him in and figured he might as well crash there, in the executive office downstairs.

Sean went upstairs and Andy lay down on the office's new Oriental throw rug. Lanier was probably upstairs too, asleep or being spoken for.

Andy was sorry he didn't have his acne medication with him, but then again, he thought, it was for the best, since he wouldn't want to discolor such an expensive-looking rug.

Sean came downstairs in a pair of white underpants. He lay on top of Andy.

"Kiss me," he said. His breath smelled like fresh toothpaste. It was nice that he'd gotten all the throw-up out of his mouth. "Kiss me."

Andy stayed stomach-down on the carpet, motionless, not sure what to do. Here was this beautiful boy lying on top of him asking to be kissed. He thought of Lanier and that it just wasn't right to make out with the boss's boyfriend, no matter how good he looked. It wasn't as though he had a precedent—Mr. Houston at the Burger Chef had a wife, not a boyfriend, and she had never come on to Andy. He just knew it would be wrong to kiss Sean.

"Why won't you kiss me?" Sean's head was so close to Andy all he could see were lips.

"I just can't do this to Lanier."

"He doesn't care."

"I just can't."

"No one will kiss me tonight," Sean said with a foreign accent. His lips were pouted. "I am *so* lonely."

After Sean left, Andy masturbated, finally thinking of someone other than Ryan.

Andy didn't have any makeup to put on in the morning, but he remembered Sheila kept a bottle in the bathroom. It was only a couple of shades darker than his; it was fortunate that she was a light-skinned black person. She said bitchy black women used to call her "yellow."

Sheila saw Andy and said, "What are you doing messing with my foundation? You look like a fool with that on your face."

"You haven't seen me without it."

"You'd *look* better if you didn't *feel* that way," she said. "Accept yourself as you are."

"That's easy for you to say. You're flawless."

"I happen to have bunions."

Before Andy could try to explain how that was different, Sean walked through the office, acting as if nothing had happened. He was headed toward the backyard pool in a skimpy bathing suit with the flags of several different nations on it. He said "Good morning" in a formal tone.

"He *is* a good-looking young man," Sheila said.

Andy didn't bring up the night before. Sean was fucked up then, it didn't count. It wasn't a breakthrough.

Sheila must have sensed something. She looked Andy up and down with wrinkles on her forehead and a frown on her mouth.

"Aren't those the same clothes you wore yesterday? And why *do* you have my makeup on?"

Andy told her.

"I told you not to mess with these people after work. You know all the coke they're on. Suppose Lanier gets caught and we have to testify. I don't want to touch the stuff. I want to be able to say, 'Why, I *certainly* had *no* idea that Mr. Ocram or the young apprentice with whom he lived partook in *illegal* drugs! Why, I thought he was happy-go-lucky from the increase in subscribers to his newsletter.'"

Andy thought Sheila was smart, but he figured his résumé was already no good because of screwing up at Burger Chef. The FBI and CIA check those things if you run for high political office. Besides, now that Andy was a journalist he figured he was allowed to have interesting experiences.

ONE morning when Lanier was up and in a good mood, he had pastries delivered to the "corporate staff."

"He must have gotten him one of those fine-looking boys from the Chesapeake House," Sheila said while she picked the sugared apricot from the pastry.

Chesapeake House was located near the D.C. bus station. A lot of boys danced on the bar there in their underpants, sometimes pulling out their penises if they were good-size or if they were on a drug that made them more forward. The clientele, mostly older gentlemen, would put bills in the briefs. Andy couldn't imagine how the older guys would tip them if they were stark naked. After the revue ended, the boys would mill around in the crowd and the men would ask them what they were doing after work.

Andy had a hard time picturing Lanier in these places. He couldn't see him anywhere other than at his word processor, hunched over in his old leather chair. Drinking fruit punch, in his underwear. Eating soggy microwaved bacon. Snorting cocaine—especially when Sheila wasn't around—straight from a big bowl filled with the stuff, still chunky. He'd stick his butter knife right into the bowl—the same knife he'd just used to make a "peenie butter" and jelly sandwich on spongy white bread—then

bring it to his nose and inhale. A third of it would fall
between the keys of his computer keyboard, a third would
stick on his nose or the stubble above his upper lip, and a
third would make him more creative, as he analyzed polls
and talked to important people about who the next president would be and why.

Meanwhile, Andy would be downstairs answering the
phone and filing papers. He got to say "One moment,
please" to a lot of senators and governors. His favorite
things to file were the canceled checks. There would be
about seven checks a month made out to boys with first
names ending in *y*—Billy, Tommy, Freddy. The endorsement on the back of each check was always an ornate,
celebrity-style signature, and right underneath would be
ID and license information: age / height / weight / eye
and hair color. Andy would try to put the information
together on the ones he hadn't run in to in the morning
and imagine what they looked like.

Of all Lanier's boys, Andy's favorite was Ricky, twenty-
one years old, six-foot-two, 160 pounds, black hair, black
eyes. He wondered what Ricky did when he wasn't with
Lanier. Maybe he was a journalist-to-be, like Andy,
chronicling the underworld for a student newspaper. Or
putting his mother, a widow without a high school di-
ploma, through night school.

Every evening Andy worked as late as he could looking
up voting percentages in *The Almanac of American Politics*,
hoping to see someone, maybe Ricky, or get invited to
something. But around seven Lanier would always say, "I
don't want to be accused of running a sweatshop," and tell
him to go home. He'd stay long enough to see Lanier lock
his wallet and the pure coke in an office file cabinet.

Andy hated going home. There was no air-
conditioning, no free food, no political posters. Once the
landlady had Andy's money she lost all interest in keeping

the place up or keeping her tenant happy. For two weeks
the toilet wouldn't flush, and every time Andy complained she'd say, "Hold it in," and slam her door in his
face.

Lanier started to like Andy more and more, even
though he wasn't his type physically.

"At first I thought you were the Young Democrat
type," Lanier said. "Then I thought you were a granola
type; then, the type that would carry a briefcase that plays
music—what's that called?"

"A beat box," Andy said.

"A beat box. Now I don't know what you are."

Andy took that as a compliment, since Lanier made a
substantial living categorizing voters.

Lanier was talking as he waded in his pool. He had lost
so much weight that it looked like he had an old woman's
big boobs. There was enough skin for two people. Andy
wished he could peel it off like a scab. Sometimes extra-fat
people might look better if they stayed that way, at least
when their clothes were off, Andy thought. The funny
thing was, Lanier didn't seem to care at all. Andy was
afraid Lanier's bathing suit was going to fall right off.
Sheila said it was sorry that a man as rich and successful as
Lanier didn't take care of himself physically. "You *know*
those men don't use that pool for laps when we're not
around."

While Lanier talked, Andy sat at the side of the pool
with just his feet in the cool water. This was the first
summer he wore makeup, and Mary Alice hadn't warned
him how much it would run in the heat. So he wore black
shirts to keep the makeup stains less obvious, and powder
over the foundation. Andy hadn't immersed his whole
body, bare except for swimming trunks, in a pool in he
couldn't remember how long. He used to wade in chlo-
rine water with his mother. She'd have on a bathing cap, a

nose plug, and earplugs. But they stopped going when she started wearing a wig.

Lanier asked, "What makes you think you're gay?"

Andy told him about Ryan, and how he was the epitome of male beauty, and how he was in love with him and thought about him all the time except at work. Andy didn't want Lanier to think he wasn't concentrating on keeping track of his laundry tickets, or making up his grocery list, or getting his favorite flavor of sorbet.

"Well, bring Ryan over," Lanier said, only half kidding. "We'll work on him."

Then Andy said he was going home to North Carolina for the Fourth of July and maybe he'd see Ryan, even though they hadn't talked since Andy left.

Lanier got out of the pool. He didn't have a towel, so he just dried himself with the pair of pants he'd left under the little yellow-striped umbrella. He knocked off his glasses with the belt buckle as he dried his hair, and Andy put them back on for him.

He looked at Andy and said, "Sean told me the other day about what happened." Then he went inside and brought back a copy of a book by a famous man who wrote about what it was like growing up gay. The guy had written it using a pseudonym, but Lanier told Andy what his real name was; he and Aaron knew each other.

"I'm having people over Sunday, you should come. I know a handsome guy who works on the Hill who's from North Carolina. Maybe we can make your Ryan jealous."

ANDY put on linen pants and a blue print shirt with a designer label. He had no trouble getting his contact lens in, and he took that as a good omen. He had gotten contact lenses just before leaving North Carolina. He was excited about having them, but when he went to pick them up he couldn't get them in. He was embarrassed in front of the optician. "That's all right, don't sweat it," the eye technician said as Andy walked out of the office still in glasses. Andy hoped Ryan could put them in for him. Ryan tried, but Andy blinked just when they were almost in.

Now that he could get both in, he realized he looked better in his mirror when he wore only one. He threw his left contact away so he wouldn't even be tempted to have $^{20}/_{20}$ vision.

Andy had let himself into Lanier's a hundred times. This time he thought it would be proper if he didn't let himself in with his key, but he was too nervous to ring the bell. He kept walking around the block. One of the neighbors peered at him suspiciously from behind a curtain. Her cat had been stolen, and there were notices stuck on all the telephone poles, mailboxes, and parked cars.

Andy went and sat on a stone bench in front of a church until he finally got up his courage. Sean answered the door. He cocked his head and said, "Welcome." He was with some French guy named Pascal who had modeled thong underwear in *GQ*. Andy was afraid his makeup was running. A quick look in the mirror reassured him it wasn't. The air-conditioning was turned pretty cold, so Andy had nothing to worry about.

All the men in the living room glanced at him quickly and smiled but then went back to whatever they were doing. Andy went into the kitchen. He knew he'd have to stay there awhile, until he felt more comfortable. Two youngish guys, one who worked for a pollster, the other for a congressman, were putting eggs and bread crumbs into raw hamburger and forming the mixture into phallic shapes. Another guy had finished arranging slices of rare roast beef and some kind of garnish on a platter and was cleaning blueberries in the sink. Andy was used to being in charge in the kitchen, making Lanier's fruit punch from concentrate, washing his dishes.

"Need any help?" he asked.

"Nah, everything's under control."

The men in the living room were already in pairs or groups of three and didn't even look up when Andy came back. He ran to the kitchen again.

"Really, let me help."

"Okay." The guy washing the blueberries left.

Andy plucked the little stems out of the blueberries, taking his time. He told the guys who were making penis—and now anus—hamburgers about a girl he'd known in high school. Her mother drank too much and she would drive out in the middle of the night to the Winn-Dixie and buy day-old blueberry pies on special. She would come home, put the pie in the oven, and wake up her daughter saying, "Wake up and eat pie!" and pretend she had just baked it.

"Really?" said the phallic guy.

"Oh?" said the anal one.

They started talking about the endive salad.

Andy finished cleaning the blueberries, but then nobody else needed him, so he cleaned them again. He thought a third cleaning might be too obvious, so he risked offering to set the table.

"It's a buffet."

"Why don't you have a drink?" somebody said.

"Brandy Alexander," said Andy.

That got a laugh. He was handed a gin and tonic and drank it down real quick, had another. He went over and sat cross-legged on the floor next to the guy from North Carolina that Lanier was going to fix him up with. The fellow was talking about foreign affairs with a congressman. Andy couldn't add anything to the conversation.

The North Carolina man was older but handsome, and after his third gin and tonic Andy got forward and moved a little closer, right by his feet. He could have touched the soles of his shoes.

Then the man and the congressman started talking about North Carolina politics. Andy knew he should say *something*.

"I fell in love with the governor's wife."

There was silence, until somebody said, "Then you're at the wrong party!" and there was laughter.

Andy felt like he'd gotten a big zit inside his throat and went downstairs to the office, where he was safe. He started filing things. Lanier came down; it was the first time Andy had seen him there.

"What's wrong?"

"I just can't say anything. I feel like a fool. The music teacher in junior high used to stare straight at me when he played that Beatles song 'Fool on the Hill.' "

"I don't know that song," Lanier said. "But there's nothing wrong with just watching, taking it in. There were times when I was working for the senator, like when he met with Sadat, when I didn't say a word, just listened."

"This isn't a foreign summit, it's a social event," Andy said.

Then Lanier took out a vial of coke from a pocket of his bunched-up pants. He spread a line on Andy's desk. Lanier gave him a straw, the same one the other fellows had been using upstairs to get high from inhaling between Lanier's word processor keys. Andy put an index finger to one nostril, the clear plastic straw up the other. It went in.

Andy felt like the pimple inside his throat had been popped, then remembered what he had learned about drugs: They mostly just heighten what you already feel, so when he took acid with Ryan he felt uglier and more hopeful, and now with the coke he was a little more clearheaded about his awkwardness.

Andy wanted to kiss Lanier, to thank him. Until now he'd wanted to kiss only pretty boys. But now he would have done it, if he could, right on top of Lanier's head.

"Come on," Lanier said. "Maybe we can fix you up with the congressman." They went back to the party.

Andy took one bite of his hamburger and looked up from his plate. To his right Sean and Pascal were caressing each other, straight ahead of him Lanier was talking about the Senate race in Arizona, and to his left the hamburger guys from the kitchen were talking about a "*gorgeous*" waiter at the Hamburger Hamlet. Andy told Lanier he needed to lie down.

"Fine," he said.

Andy fled to the guest bedroom.

He took a pillow from the foldout bed and clung to it. The walls were so white; with the air-conditioning and the coke they became perfectly clean, almost porcelain. He tried to cry but couldn't.

In the morning there was a bunch of bloody roast beef left on the buffet table. Food and drink, empty bottles were all over the place. It looked like a good time, Andy thought. He'd been invited to this.

He cleaned up. It gave him a sense of accomplishment to make the kitchen counter so clean after all this.

"Do you believe that shit upstairs?" Sheila asked Andy. "People are hungry in this city, and we've got to throw out fine meat, just because he's too lazy to put it in the refrigerator."

Then she came out of the corporate bathroom, gagging.

"I don't take his shit and I'm not about to flush it." She called Lanier up in his bedroom, woke him, told him to come downstairs to "take care of a pressing personal matter."

"Come on, Andy, we're going for a walk," she said.

They walked through the neighborhood, past the well-kept three-story town houses, and Sheila said, "It's a shame that man has such a big house all to himself." She suggested they could play a trick on Lanier by inviting all the neighbors over to his house for a big barbecue. " 'Bring the kids along! Mr. Ocram will be giving out political coloring books,' that's what the invitation would say." It would bring Lanier down to earth, she said, since all he cared about were famous people and pretty boys.

Andy pictured some mean, gruff gay man high on coke having to serve burgers to little children saying, "I want cheese on mine! Where's the Pepsi? Where's my coloring book?" He laughed but told Sheila they shouldn't do it, maybe they'd get fired.

THE first thing Andy thought of when he woke up was still Ryan; he couldn't control what he thought about that early in the morning. He had hoped that by moving away from him the opposite would happen, that maybe he would think of breakfast food instead.

By the time the Fourth of July weekend came he was ready to go home a new man: one contact lens, a new mirror image of himself, a different texture of makeup, cooler clothes, and a brand of sunglasses he was sure they didn't sell in North Carolina.

The day before he left, Andy ran some errands for Lanier. He got him a thousand dollars in cash and went to a fancy restaurant to get his hunks of rocky cocaine from the maître d', who was in his thirties and one of those blond guys everybody probably loved when he was

158

younger. He got irritated when Andy started counting out the hundred-dollar bills on the bar during lunch. "Just take it," he said with clenched teeth, and handed Andy a big yellow envelope. Andy got back into the cab; he was smart enough to have told the cabbie to wait.

While Andy ground up the coke, Lanier said, "Go ahead and take some for you and your friend." He didn't even turn around to see how much Andy took; he was hard at work at his word processor, writing.

Either he loves me or he's really into his work, Andy thought.

ANDY had been on a plane only a few times before. He'd never been afraid of being searched, but this time it was all he could think about. Before he left for the airport, he took a piece of plain white typing paper, poured the coke onto it, and folded it up. Then he put the little packet into a Publishers Clearing House Sweepstakes envelope addressed "Occupant," sealed it with Scotch tape, and stuffed it back into his pocket. This way, he could just say he had found the envelope and was going to put it into the next mailbox he saw.

As he approached the security walk-through in the airport, he remembered what his mother had said about toll-booth collectors: "Don't be too friendly, or they'll think you're making fun of them."

Andy started wishing he hadn't dressed so new wave to impress Ryan; he probably stood out more to these security people.

The uniformed ladies looked at Andy, and he gave them a forced smile, showing most of his teeth. He made sure he had good posture. He walked through the metal detector.

Beep.

"Any keys, sir?"

Andy checked. He'd forgotten them.

"Change?"

He took out two quarters.

"Try again, sir."

Beep.

And again.

Andy thought about that movie in which an American boy was busted for carrying hash through an airport in Turkey. He had taped it to his muscular chest, but he got caught and was forced to stay in a Turkish prison, despite the fact that a congressman addressed his case in the House of Representatives.

Suddenly Andy realized what it was: the container of the new makeup he was using had a fancy metal top. All the ladies who sold this makeup wore white smocks and had even whiter skin; they looked like beautiful scientists. They even had a complexion computer to tell you what shade to get. Andy had told the makeup lady that he was in television and needed it for occupational purposes.

"What is this?" the security lady asked, holding the expensive bottle of concealer.

"A gift for my mother."

"Mm-mm," she said, and waved him through.

Andy's seat was at the front of the plane. A lot of the passengers who walked past him to get to their seats had seen what he had gone through. He kept his eyes on the instructions on the vomit bag.

The fat man next to Andy was reading the row's only copy of the in-flight magazine. The man's double chin touched the lapel of his pin-striped suit as he read. Andy recognized him: it was Grady Bailey, Hainus Rainwater's campaign manager.

Once somebody from Governor Cheshire's campaign, "makin' fun' and bein' ugly," wrote up a menu for a fake dinner in honor of Grady. It had to be typed on extra-long paper to list all the foods. The bread listing alone was: Parker House rolls, buttermilk biscuits, garlic bread, light bread, sourdough (choice of three). Andy sneered at Grady, but he didn't seem to notice, and Andy ended up giving him his airline-dinner roll.

"Why, thank you, young man," Grady said.

When he got to his parents' house, Andy asked for his cat, Mittens, but was told she had died because his father had put too much flea powder on her.

"The creature was about to itch itself to death anyways," he said.

"Oh." Andy went through the list of all the important people he got to put on hold for Lanier, all the people his mother had read about or even seen on the news.

"That's nice," was all she said.

Andy excused himself and called Ryan. The line was busy, so he had the operator make an emergency interruption.

Ryan's voice had some life in it, which meant he either was happy to hear from Andy or was on some new drug that didn't give him a cotton mouth.

Ryan said, "Oh wow, it's you. Come on over, my parents are out of town."

For the first time, Andy felt comfortable driving a car. He didn't care now if mean high school girls grimaced at him at stoplights, and he didn't even glance at his skin in the rearview mirror. He looked at the road, even drove a couple of miles over the speed limit.

Ryan's hair had grown all the way out. He had bangs that covered one of his eyes completely, and he had to shake his head every few minutes to get it out. Ryan's hooded sweatshirt reminded Andy of the boys' track team in high school; his medium-size earring reminded Andy that Ryan was no longer on it.

161

Ryan hugged Andy; Andy had forgotten how small Ryan was.

"You finally got your contacts in!" Ryan said. "You look good."

"Yeah, yeah."

Ryan went to get some drinks. He had left a letter on the end table in the living room. It was from a girl in Atlanta, who wrote: "You are such a HUNK and the BEST dancer I've ever seen. My girlfriends like you a lot, too. But I saw you first. Ha-ha. Come see me when you're back in town. XXX Darya." Andy was used to it.

Ryan got a phone call. Andy was surprised when he said, "I can't talk, my friend from Washington is here." All of a sudden Andy was cool because he lived in D.C., a major city, even though Charlotte was the largest city in the Carolinas.

Andy showed Ryan what he had brought from Washington. He spilled the coke out of the Publishers Clearing House Sweepstakes envelope onto the coffee table, right by a picture of Ryan's parents on their wedding day.

"Wow, this is amazing," Ryan said.

They smoked a joint; then Ryan cut up the coke with one of his father's razor blades. "I've got acid," he said.

Andy thought Ryan never wanted to do acid with him again. Maybe he'd changed.

They rolled up a ten-dollar bill and did all the coke in one sitting, then put the tabs of acid on their tongues. As they swallowed the last bit of blotter, Ryan said he was taking Andy to the Odyssey, a gay club. Andy had seen it on the local news years before as part of a series the weatherman did, "Perversion in Charlotte," probably because he was trying to get promoted to a regular anchorman position. Maybe cool straight people went there now, Andy thought.

The club smelled like the one in Washington: cologne,

cigarettes, sweat. But there was no disco-machine smoke and the guys weren't as slick. There was no kissing on both sides of the cheek; there were a lot more flannel shirts.

Ryan ordered screwdrivers for them from a guy who said, "I'm your cock-tail waitress," and gave Ryan a long look. Ryan squeezed Andy's hand. The Ys in the neon "Odyssey" sign were throbbing. Andy wasn't sure if it was his imagination.

Andy didn't remember what happened first, but Ryan's mouth tasted like sweet oranges. Then they got in the car to drive home. They ended up kissing in the parking lot. "We can't do this here," Andy said.

The headlights merged with the streetlights; all the traffic lights turned pink and purple. Andy thought maybe they were about to become "holiday tragedies," as the newscasters call people who are killed in accidents on the Fourth of July weekend. A big truck pulled up next to them and Andy smiled and pulled his arm down, gesturing to the driver to honk his air horn. The guy said something about killing faggots. Fine, Andy thought. Ram us. To die by Ryan's side would be divine.

Ryan's parents' bed was king-size, so he and Andy decided to use it instead of his. Andy was smart enough not to look in the mirror before he got into bed. They kissed with their tongues and Ryan let Andy feel under his shirt for the first time, but he never took an article of clothing off. Ryan turned into lots of different political figures. When he was Spiro Agnew or Earl Butz, Andy would say, "Love conquers all," and he would become a Kennedy.

Andy thought Ryan's front lawn might get trenched if anybody found out about this, but then he remembered they were already high school graduates.

The next day there was no need to change the sheets,

but they cleaned the residue of the white powder off the living room table. Ryan's parents would be returning home late that afternoon. Ryan didn't want to walk Andy to his car, so he kissed him good-bye inside. "I'm going back to bed."

Andy's mother was looking out the living room window as he pulled into the driveway.

"Where were you?"

"At Ryan's."

"Why the hell didn't you call?"

"I'm sorry. We fell asleep watching the late movie."

"Jesus Christ, your father thought the car was wrecked."

"It's not, but I'm sorry." The remnants of illegal drugs mellowed Andy; he didn't want to fight. Besides, his dream had come true. His tongue had entered Ryan's mouth, and vice versa. There was love in the world, reason to have faith.

They were eating a late breakfast. Andy sat in his old chair at the kitchen table.

"Your grandfather worked as a mortician during the Depression," Andy's mother said. "He had to make people up before they were laid out for viewing."

"Yeah?" Andy said.

"And I want to tell you, you look like a G-D corpse with that makeup on."

His father agreed.

"Better a corpse than a crater face," he said. "You know, you could use some makeup yourself, Mom."

Andy didn't stay for dessert.

ANDY'S parents were in a bad mood, but they had to put on for the neighborhood Fourth of July party. Andy's

164

mother made her "world-famous" potato salad and cole slaw for her contribution. Walking over to the cul-de-sac where the party was with her two big Tupperware containers, she grumbled, "I don't like any of these losers. But what if your grandmother ever needs a ride to the hospital when we're not home?"

Jerry and Neeta Mitchell from the house next door set off some fireworks they had gotten just past the South Carolina border; in North Carolina they were illegal. Everybody clapped. Andy ate a tube steak that tasted like grill gas.

"Now, you're living in Washington, is that right?" a neighbor lady asked.

"Yes ma'am."

"Well, why in the world would you want to go up there?"

And Andy remembered.

LANIER asked Andy how things had gone down in North Carolina.

"Boy, that coke really did the trick," Andy said. Now he knew how football players felt when they talked about getting a piece. Lanier smiled and snorted another line.

That night Andy called Ryan from Lanier's house. "How do you feel about it?" Andy whispered.

"Um, I don't know."

"Are your parents in the room?"

"No."

"Can you talk?"

"I mean yeah, my mom's here, I've got to go."

Andy went out to a gay disco, the Fraternity House. He waited until closing time when the lights would come on and somebody, out of desperation, would take him home.

The guy tried to fuck him but it didn't work. He lived out in the suburbs, by the vice-president's house, and was pissed off. So when it came time to leave, he didn't want to drive Andy all the way home. He dropped him off at a bus stop underneath a sign that said "Welcome to Washington."

Andy's mother had always told him, "Never call someone more than twice in a row. You'd be making a damn fool of yourself." Finally this advice paid off. Ryan called.

He had been fired from his job at the hospital, caught with a joint. He said the administration people didn't believe his story that he was taking it to the cancer ward. "My mom's giving me a lot of shit. Can I come up?"

"You know you can, Ryan."

"I'll be there in eight hours."

Ryan arrived still in his hospital orderly's uniform. It was soft, like pajamas. They collapsed on Andy's bed. Andy felt another boy's groove thing for the first time. Ryan came and fell asleep.

My life has been validated, Andy thought.

10

ANDY and Ryan went out to the 9:30 Club. It was video night, so there were music videos to dance to all night long—no live thrasher bands. Before going, they put on their makeup together at the bathroom mirror. All Ryan used was eyeliner, but he didn't even need that. Andy couldn't keep his hands off him. In his mind he kept seeing those dorm-room bunk beds. I've got a lot of time to make up for, he thought.

They danced together. Ryan was a much better dancer. He could put his hands to his head and pretend he was going crazy and move his feet at the same time. After a while Andy went to the wall and watched Ryan dance by himself. A guy in a black fishnet shirt and leather pants started dancing with him. When the music changed the guy went to the black bathroom, which smelled like pee, got a paper towel, and came back to wipe Ryan's brow.

Andy had always thought that at least with Ryan straight he'd never have to compete with another guy for his attention. This was the worst.

Ryan exchanged phone numbers with the other guy.

"What were you doing with that guy?"

"Dancing. Duh."

"I could see that."

"He works at that punk boutique in Georgetown. I'm gonna model for them in their ads."

Ryan did not let Andy touch him that night, or the next. He would say "Cut it out" and then fall asleep, or at least pretend to.

Andy wasn't allowed to touch the most beautiful boy in the world, and he slept right next to him every night. So he bought some sleeping pills.

He took triple the amount recommended and fell into a hard sleep. He woke up with an awful headache, worried he'd maybe snored or drooled. It was late afternoon, and Ryan had already showered and dressed. He was wearing black leather pants, a T-shirt, and suspenders that the guy from the punk boutique had given him.

"Where are you going?" Andy asked.

"A party," Ryan said.

"Can I come?" He hated himself as soon as he asked.

"Um, it's kind of private."

It turned out a tenant from across the hall heard Ryan yell, "I'm not putting out for you every night." So he told the landlady, "Either the fags go or all the rest of us go. We won't live in a house with a bunch of fags!"

The landlady told Andy to get out, that she never said he was allowed to have a roommate.

"You've forfeited your security deposit, too."

"That's not fair."

"Take me to court, see what the judge says. Sodomy is illegal in the District of Columbia."

Andy hadn't even done it, but he didn't want to be put on trial.

Ryan said he was going to move out anyway. He had

gotten a job waiting tables at a fancy restaurant, so he could afford to split. There was no place for Andy to go but Lanier's.

LANIER was writing a book of behind-the-scenes anecdotes of political campaigns. *Baby-Kissers, Mudslingers, and Whistleblowers: The Real Campaign Trail* was a tell-all exposé. It contained rare gossip that had never even appeared in *Inside D.C.* about presidential campaigns and important races for senator and governor. It had little-known bizarre tales that had been hushed up for years, like the one about the presidential candidate who hired his brother as campaign manager. The only trouble was, his brother had been stone dead for a number of years. But the candidate felt he could still communicate with him and get the shrewd advice his brother had taken with his corpse to the grave. This made the deputy campaign manager furious, since he was second in line for everything—office space, staff, salary—to a dead man. The dead brother had a living secretary who had no work to do; she just waited by the phone for calls that never came.

The book had been signed up by a tough woman editor in New York who answered the phone, "What do you want?" which Andy had a hard time not taking personally. "Lanier Ocram calling, ma'am," he'd say. But if Andy didn't get Lanier on the line quickly enough, she'd always hang up, even if it was just seconds. Anyway, after she saw Lanier's completed manuscript, she said it was "the stuff of after-dinner speeches," and the project was canned.

Lanier was high-strung to begin with, and when he got this news, he threw his word processor across the room.

At the Wang service center, it was embarrassing enough for Andy to be asked about the powder between the keys.

"What is this white substance?" the computer service-man asked, squinting at Andy through thick-lensed glasses.

"I don't know, I think it's flea powder," Andy answered.

It was obvious the damage was "owner-inflicted," so it wouldn't be covered by the warranty.

When Andy returned to the office, he yelled the news to Lanier, who was in his bedroom upstairs. He came running down, wearing a T-shirt and baggy pants that he held up with his hands. He told Andy to get the president of Wang on the phone. When he grabbed the receiver from Andy, he started yelling, "Listen, I know important people, senators, governors," and his pants fell down. His penis was small.

The president of Wang and Lanier had met at a corporate briefing Lanier had given in Tokyo. He assured Lanier he'd do everything in his power to get him a new word processor.

Pacified, Lanier lay down on the corporate sofa and started drawing circles in the air with his index finger. He said that since Sean had left (Lanier wouldn't buy him a new motorbike) and his book had been rejected, he was in bad shape. "It's an awful time to be alone," he said. Andy was worried he might have to see this grown man cry.

"I need something to cuddle at night, something that will always be there for me," Lanier decided.

Andy had to look through the *Washington Post* classifieds to find Lanier a dog.

Andy made a couple of calls, got an address, and Lanier drove out to pick up his new pet. He came back with two yippy dogs named Hubert and Lyndon that he bought from a rich lady in the suburbs.

Lanier was so proud he invited the neighbors over to ooh and aah over them. He even started talking baby talk to the critters. But as happy as Lanier seemed to be, Andy knew, when he knelt down to cover the floor with newspaper, that Lanier would lose interest quickly. He wouldn't be talking baby talk to them for long.

Soon enough it got to the point that the dogs were forbidden to go upstairs; they had to stay locked in the bathroom or in the office with Andy and Sheila. Sheila brought in air freshener, but the combination of its spring bouquet scent and the smell of dog poop made Andy the worst kind of sick. He wanted to throw up but couldn't.

Lanier told Andy that if he couldn't keep the dogs under control, he'd have to hire a dog trainer. So Andy looked through the yellow pages and called a few professional dog trainers to come over and interview for the job.

When the first trainer, Mr. Sarmast, showed up, Lanier told Andy it was *his* problem, so he'd better take care of it. Mr. Sarmast was the cheapest one who'd advertised. He came with a bunch of brochures, all of which opened with his slogan: "I Keep Cats from Purring and Dogs from Barking!" But he did not say how, only that the animals would have to spend a night at his place. Andy didn't know what to ask him—he had never had to interview anybody for a job before—so he took the literature and said he'd think it over.

The next trainer, Mrs. Enelow, held her nose the minute she was in the room and left soon after, saying, "These aren't show dogs, they don't need a trainer. All they need, honey, is some love and attention."

By the time the man who got the job came by, Andy was ready to hire anybody who'd stay. Mr. Spence brought with him a portfolio, with photographs of D.C. celebrities and their dogs—trained by him. After they'd gone through Mr. Spence's portfolio, Andy told him he had the job, but that Mr. Ocram probably wouldn't pose for a photo.

The next day, he came back to walk the dogs with Andy and teach him how to get them to heel. Across the street, Mr. Jones stood watching from his porch. His German shepherd, Luger, was very well trained, but then again, Mr. Jones always carried a birch switch, which he said was the same one he'd used on his son LeMont, who now worked as a lawyer on K Street. He was shaking his head and the switch and yelling, "That's no way to train a hound, Andy!" Mr. Spence left after half an hour and handed Andy a bill for seventy-five dollars.

Even with Mr. Spence's professional services there was no real improvement. The smell just got worse and worse. One time the creatures ate the tape inside a cassette and pooped it out. And Lanier said their yipping kept him up all night.

Lanier started accusing Andy of trying to take over *Inside D.C.*

"Lanier, I'm nineteen years old, nobody even knows me. Don't be crazy."

"Don't play dumb with me, you're working for the competition. I've been watching your activities for a long time! The proof's in the pudding, y'know."

He told Andy if he called him crazy one more time, he'd send him back to the farm. "I'm not crazy, it's *you* who ought to go to the hospital. I know you're hoarding my stationery."

Andy started having to cancel Lanier's speeches at the last minute. He would call the organizers, who not only had collected a lot of money to hear Lanier speak but had booked hotel buffet rooms and advertised for the events weeks in advance. "I'm sorry, Mr. Ocram isn't feeling well." The person on the other end would always be upset, and one guy started yelling about how he wished he had scheduled Paul Harvey or an inspirational speaker.

Andy thought about getting a real job on Capitol Hill

or maybe with the Democratic National Committee. But somehow he couldn't bring himself even to go for interviews.

Everything was making him feel so sick he didn't even try to see Ryan, who had moved into an apartment in the Hispanic part of town. The thought of kissing someone, even Ryan, made him feel sicker still. He went to a doctor, the first he'd seen since the dermatologist.

When he saw how tall Andy was, the doctor said, "Well, you must be some basketball player!" The idea of jumping around after a bouncing basketball made Andy swallow hard. The doctor handed him a prescription for antinausea pills.

Andy had to ask Sheila if he could borrow twenty dollars for the prescription; he was broke. He told her Lanier would pay her back, since it was for a job-related illness.

She looked at him suspiciously as she pulled the money from her clutch bag, saying, "All right then."

Andy ran to the pharmacy. He didn't wait until he got back to work, he took the pills right then and there. Since he felt so nauseated, he took three more than recommended. Then he headed over to the Safeway to pick up some dog food and a new apple-pectin brand of rug freshener.

Standing in the express lane, he realized his jaw was tightening. As he moved in line he felt weirder and weirder. Muscles in his jaw that he didn't even know existed were going haywire. Andy wondered if other people could see it. He hoped the lady at the register wouldn't ask how he was today or whether he had coupons, because he couldn't tell what would come out if he tried to talk.

He felt in his pocket to make sure he had his keys, then walked to Lanier's quickly. Passing by the gourmet cheese shop, he noticed a boy in a white smock behind the counter. He was beautiful to Andy, even though he had a hearing aid. Andy couldn't stand the idea of losing it in front of him.

He got to Lanier's and was afraid he couldn't talk. Sheila was out to lunch. Ryan was at work, waiting tables, so he couldn't call him. He called a deli delivery place but all he could get out were gurgles and heavy breathing. "Please, leave me in peace," a man with a foreign accent said. Suddenly Andy found himself writhing in pain, rolling on the floor in fetal position. He called 911, hoping they wouldn't think it was a prank phone call. He gurgled out, "I need a doctor," and sputtered out the address. Thank God this city had simple names for its streets instead of long names like Cherry Grove Hill or Cedar Crest Valley Road.

Two big black men in light blue uniforms with reflective orange armbands came. He handed one of them the prescription pill bottle and held up five fingers to indicate how many he'd taken. They took his pulse, checked his blood pressure, and put him on a stretcher, all the while yakking about a sporting event.

When they got to the emergency room, the nurse knew right away what was wrong. She said Andy was "a real Johnny-on-the-spot" to bring that pill bottle along and she wished all her patients were so smart. She gave him some kind of injection, told him never to take more than the prescribed amount of any medication, and sent him on his way. He was a little lightheaded but at least didn't feel that he had to throw up.

It was only midafternoon, time for Lanier's snack, so Andy went back over and fixed him his afternoon treat, Kool-Aid and a bacon and butter sandwich.

Lanier was playing with his new word processor. Without looking up, he said he had paid Sheila the twenty dollars.

174

LANIER'S interior decorators owed him a favor, so when he asked, they said it would be okay for his assistant to sleep in their guest room for a low monthly price.

Both of them had a skinny mustache and a skinny body, which made it hard to tell them apart. Andy heard them fucking and wondered if they had the same problem.

Dencil and Herbert had met waiting for a hotel elevator in Portland when they were each there on a business trip.

"So if you two had been given rooms on different floors, you would have never met?" Andy asked.

"Yes, isn't it amaaazing?" Dencil replied.

Every room in their house was immaculate. Andy was afraid of messing things up, so he stayed put in his room. He bought some plastic glasses at the Safeway when Dencil and Herbert complained that he'd left cloudy residue on a glass of theirs he had used. "Just a friendly warning," they said in unison.

ONE day Sheila told Andy that Lanier was having more and more trouble getting out of bed. A few days later Lanier told Andy he could take over the newsletter— "That was your plan, anyway." Andy called up some of Lanier's friends and asked them to come by, to try to cheer the man up. They told Andy he ought to get him into the Betty Ford Center.

Andy went home and walked straight to his room, as usual. He was surprised to see that his bed had been made and his shades were drawn. They'd been in there. Andy immediately thought about what had happened to the mattress.

Early one morning a dampness on his thigh had woken him and he had gasped, at first thinking it was blood. But when he'd looked down and seen the big black blotch all over his leg *and* the mattress, he'd felt even worse. He'd fallen asleep while writing a piece for Lanier about off-year gubernatorial races and had left the cap off his fountain pen, which had then leaked until it was empty. He'd panicked, turned the mattress over, and figured he'd be long gone before Dencil and Herbert ever discovered it.

There was a knock on the door.

He couldn't be sure but thought it was Dencil who said, "We tried to work with you," and Herbert who handed him a big Hefty bag, saying, "We'll have to keep all of this month's rent to get a new mattress."

Everything Andy owned fit into the Hefty bag. He asked if he could make a phone call. "Is it local? And that reminds me, we'll need your new address for when we get this month's phone bill."

Ryan finally answered the phone and sighed. "If you're really in trouble, okay."

That night Andy slept with his head on Ryan's chest. Ryan didn't say anything and didn't move a muscle, not even when Andy caressed him. He has never really touched me, Andy thought.

In the morning Ryan said, "There's a spare mattress in the other room. I think you should sleep there."

There were no sheets. Andy slept on the mattress, bare.

The neighborhood was mostly Hispanic and black; there wasn't a political analyst or lobbyist for miles. Loud music from beat boxes filled the street—salsa and rap. A few blocks away, by the bus stop, was a twenty-four-hour church from which an old black man's voice preached through a megaphone-style speaker mounted outside.

It was Ryan's birthday, and Andy baked a chocolate cake from a recipe Sheila had given him. There were only plastic utensils at Ryan's apartment, so Andy made it in Lanier's kitchen. He got icing in a tube and wrote in his best calligraphy *Happy 19th.*

Andy called the Dragon's Garden, the Chinese restaurant where Lanier took all his important political friends. He reserved a table, saying it was for Lanier's nephew.

Andy ordered moo-shoo vegetables. Since they came wrapped in a pancake, he figured it would be all right if he ate with his hands. At least it would be better than trying to use chopsticks.

"Ask the waiter for a fork. You really look disgusting," Ryan said.

When the bill came and Andy told the waiter to put it on Mr. Ocram's account, the maître d' came out and quietly informed Andy the account was no longer good at the Dragon's Garden.

"I'm really sorry. I'll pay you back," Andy said to Ryan.

"Forget it, I'm going out. Thanks for the thought, Andy."

About five hours later, Ryan came home. Andy was sleeping and woke up when Ryan turned on the stereo full blast.

He was playing one of his import EPs. The song was about some woman with beautiful skin the singer had a crush on. Andy couldn't make out most of the words, but the refrain rang clear: "She had perfect skin."

Andy banged on the wall. "Could you turn it down?"

No response.

He got out of bed and slammed his door, hoping the record might skip. "Could you *please* turn it down."

No.

Andy went in to Ryan's room. Ryan was in bed, his eyes closed, his pants off.

"This is my apartment. My door is closed. Go back to your room," he said quietly and coolly.

"Asshole." Andy turned down the volume.

Ryan got up slowly and turned it back up.

Andy turned off the stereo completely. He grabbed Ryan's arm when Ryan walked over to turn it back on.

"Don't touch me!" Ryan shrieked. It was the first time he'd ever raised his voice like that.

Andy was almost aroused when he first went in and saw Ryan on the bed in his underwear, but now all he felt was hate.

He knew where Ryan kept his tips from the restaurant. He grabbed a wad of bills from his dresser drawer. It must have been at least four hundred dollars.

"I put you up when you came here! At least give me some money to get a place, if you don't want me." Andy's eyes felt hot with tears.

"Take a look at yourself," Ryan said. Andy had never seen him sneer before.

He knew his hair was messed up; after all, he'd just been woken up. And his face was splotchy with makeup and pimple lotion.

"You should see yourself," Ryan said.

Andy picked Ryan up and threw him on the hardwood floor.

Ouch.

He was surprised to find himself throwing Ryan's slim body against the floor again. He wanted to break him.

"I'm calling the fucking cops." Ryan never even tried fighting back.

Andy picked him up again, threw him down a little harder. Ryan's eyes were closed. Andy pressed his face against Ryan's chest. He was breathing. Andy looked down and saw he had gotten makeup on Ryan's white T-shirt. He took it off so he could put a clean one on him.

Ryan looked so good without a shirt. And it had been such a long time since Andy had seen him that way. He kissed Ryan's smooth olive chest all over. Touched it with his hands. He looked at his face. Perfect.

He pulled the serrated plastic knife out of the birthday cake, pressed it against Ryan's face. Andy moved the knife, sawlike, over Ryan's cheekbone. Thin white lines appeared between streaks of chocolate icing where the blade scratched the skin.

Andy continued. But before blood was drawn, he remembered what he'd always wanted: to be together with Ryan, two little boys lying flat on their stomachs, feet in the air; two beautiful boys living where the music is.

Andy put the knife down and carefully licked the chocolate off Ryan's cheek. He picked up Ryan's hand and turned the palm to his own face and forced a caress. He'd never known what that felt like.

Ryan seemed to stir. Quickly, Andy put on a new face, then crammed his belongings back into his Hefty bag. The plastic was beginning to rip. He picked a hundred dollars out of the wad of bills he'd taken from Ryan's dresser and left the rest on top of one of the stereo speakers.

He looked down at Ryan, his thick hair, the dip in the small of his back, the curve of his ass. He dropped his apartment keys next to the money.

It would be hard to find a cab this late; where would he go, anyway? Andy walked down the street. The church megaphone speaker was going full blast. Was it live or recorded? Andy tried to look in the window, but it was stained glass. Then the message stopped and an old black man stepped out the door.

"Did you hear it, young man?"

"No, I was just walking by."

Maybe he would let him in.